Death on the Trek

A People of the Wind Mystery

Kaye George

Untreed
Reads

Also by Kaye George and Untreed Reads Publishing

A Fine Kettle of Fish (ebook)

Death in the Time of Ice (ebook and print)

The Bavarian Krisp Caper (ebook)

"Henry, Gina, and the Gingerbreadhouse" in the Untreed Reads Anthology *Grimm Tales* (ebook)

"Immy Goes to the Dogs (An Imogene Duckworthy Mystery)" in the Untreed Reads Anthology *The Untreed Detectives* (ebook)

Author's Note

During the Wisconsinian glaciation, as our story begins, ice sheets are advancing across the northern part of what is now the Midwest United States. These glaciers would alter the landscape dramatically and would remain until about ten or fifteen thousand years ago.

Cold winds blew across the surface, heralding the glaciers, killing the vegetation even before the ice reached it. When the edge of the ice arrived, it uprooted everything in its path. Most of the huge animals that existed on the continent until ten thousand years ago, when they all mysteriously disappeared, retreated before the approaching ice shelf. Although some wooly mammoth and other hardy animals remained on the tundra during the last Ice Age, many more, including the shorter-haired Columbian mammoth, roamed farther south.

Anyone dependent on the megafauna for survival would have had to follow them. As in *Death in the Time of Ice*, I have taken a few liberties in this tale.

There is no evidence that Neanderthals ever lived on the American continents, although it is quite probable Homo sapiens (called Tall Ones) were here at that time. I have added other interesting beings who existed in other parts of the world: Homo floresiensis from Java, called Mikino here, and Denisovans from Siberia, called Hoodens.

I have chosen among the many conflicting theories and opinions to suit my purposes and my story. The matriarchal Neanderthals about whom you are about to read throw spears to bring down game. They have speaking abilities, but limit its use, as a middle ground between speech theories. Their main communication is done with their own special kind of telepathy.

I hope you enjoy the Hamapa tribe adventures presented in these pages.

Chapter 1

"The conquest of fire by man deservedly ranks among the most impressive of all race-memories, for perhaps no one natural agency has done so much to exalt the potency of the human race as has that which gives us heat and light and power."

—*Native American Mythology,*
Hartley Burr Alexander, p. 46

Enga Dancing Flower watched the progress of the boy who was making his way down the hill from the Holy Cave. This was the last time he would bring the fire from the small mountain to the Paved Place for the nightly meeting in their long-time home—the last time he, or any of the tribe, would ever visit the Holy Cave. For many seasons, it had been the task of Akkal to tend both the permanent fire in the Holy Cave and the community fire in the village. When rain sometimes put out that fire, the black-haired Fire Tender diligently prepared the pit at the center of the meeting place and brought new fire down before the next meeting time.

The warm and cold times cycled, as they always did, and the most warm time was coming. The night breath of Mother Sky held only a trace of chill. The birds in the woods surrounding the village were making soft peeps while they bedded down so that they could rise up again with Sister Sun, completing that cycle, and sing at full voice.

The fire Akkal carried lit his face from below, its light throwing flickering shadows across his young features and glinting off his long dark hair and eyes. Smoke trailed after him.

The leader of the tribe, Hama, the Most High Female, had summoned them after they ate their evening meal, as usual. But this was far from the usual meeting. The meal had only been a few bites, and that was not usual either. Although it took place at the normal time, soon after Sister Sun disappeared, this meeting was different.

The tribe knew that this was their last time of no sun in the place most of them had lived for all their days. Most of the huge mammoth they had always hunted had fled.

Moons ago, before this last dark season, a group of males had journeyed far enough to see the gigantic, looming field of Great Ice. It was moving, very slowly, but the movement was toward them. The animals the Hamapa tribe depended on, which were mostly mammoth, were scattering. Some had migrated toward the ice, onto the barren, frozen land that lay before it, in its path. The tribe could not live in that place. Some animals had fled to places with more warmth. That was where they would go. This decision had been made after much discussion and pondering. The decision had not been easy, but all were satisfied that it must be so. They must depart.

Every heart was heavy, every brow worried, even though they knew it was a necessary thing they would do. Everyone, males, females, children, had spent their time packing up what they would be able to carry with them. At new sun they would depart.

Enga felt the heavy sorrow. Even though each one cloaked every thought in the darkest colors of night, their grief was heavy enough to drip through. Enga looked up, almost expecting to see a black cloud of dark thoughts above the gathering. Mother Sky looked down on them with her many twinkling eyes. Brother Moon, almost at his fullest, seemed to smile and say he would be with them on their travels. The fire pit sent out a familiar warmth and the comforting smell of smoke, as it always did. These were not enough to lift the spirits of Enga.

Hama stood. Before she was elected leader, her name had been Rho Lion Hunter because she had killed a lion by herself. She was thick of body with dark, intelligent eyes. She sent out a public thought, bathed in brightest red so that everyone could receive it in their minds.

Singer will sing a Song of Asking for our long journey so that the Spirits will be kind as we travel.

Lakala Rippling Water, the Singer, started with a Song of Blessing to Mother Sky. Her voice, usually confident and fluid, wavered with fright. When she finished, she next sent a Song of Asking into the night air. She gained strength, tilting her head upward so that her trilling notes surely reached to Mother Sky and beyond, to her child, the Most High Spirit Dakadaga. The Singer asked for safety, strength, guidance, and success in finding a new home for the tribe.

When Lakala was finished, Hama stood once more and made one of her rare Official Pronouncements. The Hamapa saved oral speech for the most formal occasions. This was one such time.

"Hoody!" she exclaimed aloud, her dark eyes flashing from one to another of the tribe.

The tribe heard the word, *Listen!* The word rose to Brother Moon, as the song of Lakala had.

"Yaya, Hama vav." She shook her head and raised her face, her gleaming curls bouncing in the flickering flames.

This meant: *Yes, the Most High Female speaks.*

"Dakadaga sasa vav Akkal."

Dakadaga has given the name for Akkal.

A rippling of surprised thought went through them. At the Naming Ceremony, twenty moons after birth, all tribe members received a short name. The descriptive adult name, however, was given much later by Dakadaga through the Hama. Usually a Hamapa male had his Passage Ceremony after fifteen summers. This was where young males and females received their complete names. Enga had been given the name Enga Dancing Flower, and her birth-sister Ung had been called Ung Strong Arm.

Enga knew that Akkal had passed only fourteen summers. But if Dakadaga, the Most High Spirit, had decreed a name, it would be so. Was the Spirit worried that Akkal would not make it through the coming journey to next summer? This, then, was the reason Akkal sat nearest Hama.

Then Hama spoke the official name of Akkal. "Burmana."

It was fitting that Akkal would now be Akkal Firetender. He had started doing the job at a very young age, when the Firetender before him was not careful enough and was eaten by the flames.

A bigger shock came when Hama continued. "Dakadaga sas vav Mootak."

Dakadaga has given the name for Mootak.

Enga could smell the fear now. Akkal lacked only one summer, but Mootak lacked two. He was being named two summers early! Did Dakadaga know the tribe would fail to complete their trek? Would they not find the mammoth? Would they starve, like the Gata tribe had done?

Mootak was apprenticed to the Storyteller. Enga has listened in on many of their sessions. Panan One Eye, the oldest member of the tribe at fifty summers, carried the lore of all the Storytellers before him, going back to the Time of Crossing, and even back to the last Time of Great Ice.

All stared at Hama, trying to gain a clue about what else Dakadaga had told her.

"Tiki Kair."

Big Heart.

Enga nodded and saw that her birth-sister, Ung Strong Arm, nodded also. It fit him. He was small, like his birth-mother, Ongu Small One, and he had straight black hair, like his seed giver, Sannum Straight Hair. Sannum had been one of the favorites of Enga ever since the Hamapa tribe had taken in her and Ung. It was a good name. Sannum had a big heart and so did Mootak.

The eyes of the two young ones, still boys, but now made adults early, shone with joy and pride. It was not done for a Hamapa to think of himself before the tribe, but everyone would understand this brief moment of vanity. Enga added her warm thoughts to all of those already being directed at Akkal Firetender and Mootak Big Heart.

4

Lakala Rippling Water stood and sang Death to Childhood while the tribe listened in silence.

It was done. The tribe had two new adult males.

Now was the time for the Saga. Panan One Eye looked at Hama, for his signal to begin. The firelight played off his round, bare head, making it look as shiny as Brother Moon.

Hama did not look at Panan. She nodded at Mootak.

Mootak Big Heart stood, beaming. What a special night he was having! He had received his name—two summers early—and he would give the Saga for the first time.

Chapter 2

"Horses became extinct in the Old World at the end of early Eocene time, about 50 million years ago, but horse evolution continued in the New World. Subsequent species moved back and forth between North America and Asia..."

—*Ice Age Mammals of North America:*
A Guide to the Big, the Hairy, and the Bizarre,
Ian M. Lange, p.122

Mootak Big Heart began to relate the Saga of the Little Horses. Enga sent a short pinkish thought-burst of approval straight to him. It was a most appropriate tale for this time. His thought-speak reached every mind and went deep into every heart as he sent forth the familiar tale. It was given perfectly, exactly as Panan One Eye always gave it.

Once many small horses ran free on the plains. These horses were like the large ones that roam in herds now, like the mammoth also do, but were smaller than horses now, and very fleet.

They were eaten by large predators, and some were eaten by Hamapa, although we have always preferred to hunt slower, larger game. Our Ancient Ones began to notice there were fewer and fewer of these small horses over time. Large herds dwindled down to small ones. Then an Ancient One, who was a good tracker, saw a herd going toward the place where Sister Sun goes to sleep and followed them. Maybe this was a time when they needed food, and he wanted to hunt them. I do not know why he followed them, just that he did. They ran for many suns, then kept going for many moons.

The herd he tracked was joined by other small herds and grew large. It became a huge herd, but kept running in the same direction.

The good tracker finally had to turn around and return to his village. But he felt the horses would keep running. The Storyteller of his tribe believed that the horses were going to the place where the Hamapa came from in ancient times. They would go, he said, far to the north and across a narrow land. Then they would be in a vast land, like the one we are in. They could live there. Maybe they would not be eaten by so many large hunting animals.

The Hamapa tribe would now attempt to follow the mammoth as the ancient tracker had followed the little horses. Mootak concluded the Saga, adding a new thought of his own at the end.

Others have said the small horses traveled in the direction away from the Guiding Bear who turns with the Seasons in Mother Sky, to a land where it is always warm.

Wherever they went, they are no longer here. Sometimes creatures need to move in order to survive. This may be what the small horses have done. It is what our Ancient Ones did when they came here. And it is what we must do now.

No sound disturbed the crackling of the fire, which was dancing in the slight breeze. No thoughts were sent out. The tribe, people of muscular limbs and of small stature compared to some others, sat in a circle around the fire.

Each Hamapa was wrapped in private thoughts, cloaked in dark colors so that others could not perceive them. Enga knew, though, that these private thoughts were full of fear. She fingered the carved wooden figure she held under her mammoth skin wrap, next to the seed of her mate, Tog Flint Shaper, the seed which was growing inside her. What would the future hold for her child? She was not able to visualize it. She only knew that the life of the new baby would be vastly different than hers had been, in a different land. A land she did not know yet. She longed to touch the skin of Tog, but he was not tuned into her thoughts at this moment.

Hama rose again, rattled her gourd, and nodded to Lakala Rippling Water, the Singer. Lakala was surprised to be asked to sing again. Hama sent forth a picture of dancing and Enga gladdened. She was happy that the tribe would dance tonight, although they all must be careful not to get too tired out before the start of the trek.

As Lakala stood up, she caught the eyes of Sannum Straight Hair and Panan One Eye. Sannum set a beat on his log drum in time with the nodding of the head of Lakala. When her high, soft tones lifted into the air above them, it was another Song of Blessing to Dakadaga. After a bit, Panan raised his wooden flute and followed the notes of Lakala with trills of his own.

Having another song after the Saga was not the usual order, but, Enga mused, nothing was usual any more.

Panan had been holding Sooka, the baby of Vala Golden Hair, but handed her back to Vala when he started playing. Sooka kicked and squirmed and Vala was barely able to hold her. The green eyes of Vala showed annoyance. Enga could understand her attitude, somewhat.

This baby was not like any other Hamapa infant. She came from a seed that was not that of a Hamapa, a person very different from them. Her limbs were long and thin, and she had not walked yet, even though she had already been alive six moons. Hamapa babies, sturdier and stronger, were walking at that age. Whim, the baby of Fee Long Thrower and Bahg Swiftfeet, ran back and forth on his short, fat legs as the adults had their meeting.

A tall, pale stranger who had sojourned with them had given Vala the seed for this baby, Sooka. The Tall One had also had a narrow body and a different kind of face, the lower part of his jaw sticking out where that of the Hamapa did not. He was eventually called Stitcher because of his skill at binding together skins with a sharp bird bone and leather thongs, but he was no longer with the tribe.

When he joined them, he had brought with him buttons made of antler, a marvel that none of the Hamapa had ever seen. Stitcher was also the carver of the wooden figure Enga held tightly in this time of no sun, their last one in this place. The figure captured the curves of the female who had been Hama at the time. Enga saw her face when she gazed on the carving, her hair loose, as she had always worn it. Enga fingered the woven bracelets, set in wood. She missed Aja Hama very much. The name Aja Hama meant Former Most High Female, but it implied much more, as it was not given to all former leaders. It was given to that one in honor, after her death. This was the female who had raised her and her birth-sister when the tribe had taken them in. That leader had been cruelly slain. Enga was probably not the only one who wished she were still here to lead them on this frightening journey into unknown places.

The squirming baby nearly slipped from the arms of Vala. Tog Flint Shaper, the mate of Enga, left her side and went to help Vala. Enga clamped down tightly on her feeling of jealousy. It would not do to annoy Tog about this. Enga had always known he was attracted to the female with the beautiful golden hair and the bright green eyes. But, she reminded herself yet another time, he was *her* mate, not that of Vala. He would never stay with Vala, would not mate with her.

Lakala changed into a Song of Asking, pleading for safe passage in the moons to come. Now Hama nodded to Enga, the best dancer in the tribe.

Clad in her everyday mammoth skin, as was the rest of the tribe, Enga rose to help with the appeal to the Spirits. To make the best impression, she should have been wearing her more formal bear skin cape, but everything was packed away, ready for departure at first sun. They would leave hungry. There had been a hunt two suns ago, but not much had been caught, only a few small ground squirrels.

She tucked the carving into her waist pouch and moved gracefully around the fire, in front of the Hamapa who sat in the Paved Place. She swayed in time to the rhythm, closing her eyes to block the sight of Tog beside Vala, their heads almost touching and smiles on their faces, to block the fear in the eyes of her tribal brothers and sisters, to try to block her own fear.

It had worried her that, a few suns before the early Passage Ceremonies, Hama had also given names to Sooka and Whim.

Before this, Hamapa babies had always had the Naming Ceremony after they had passed twenty moons.

* * *

Jeek had worked so hard and the blazing fire was so warm that he was dozing off during the assembly. Earlier, his mother, Zhoo of Still Waters, had ordered him and Teek Bearclaw to do one task after another. In addition to clothing, tools, and adornments, which everyone had, she also must pack her healing supplies, for she was the Healer for the tribe. Jeek cut up a good portion from the supply of the long grasses stacked in the corner of their wipiti and tucked them into the bottom of the large pouch they would carry with them. As he worked, using the large stump in the middle of their dwelling to whack at the grasses with the flint knife, he wondered if the new place they found would have all the conveniences that this one had.

He carefully wrapped her knife in a thick scrap of mammoth hide and placed it into their large pouch. Zhoo then gave him instructions to wrap well the skin bag full of bear fat and the hollow gourd full of honey and place them on the top of the other healing supplies.

Zhoo and some others had all helped with the hardest task, getting the skins from their wipitis taken down and ready so they could depart at first sun. Pieces were cut from them to make travel pouches. Other small pieces were saved to be fashioned into foot wrappings, and sacs and pouches to carry whatever else would be needed. They all wanted to start as early as they could. The seven wipitis they dismantled were all of equal size, but the two left intact were much larger. In one had dwelt Hama and her mate, and in the other, the single males. At this dark time, they would all attempt to sleep in the two large ones, then they would dismantle them just before they left. The mammoth tusks that supported the structures would have to be abandoned, being much too heavy to carry.

Many had joked that no one would sleep during the time of no sun, but Jeek was sure he would. He was so tired.

The mammoth tusks that were being left behind marked where they had lived for so long. In the darkness, they rose from the ground like bare, white rib bones.

Now, he watched Akkal coming down the Sacred Hill, carrying the precious fire, but soon nodded off, in spite of the alarming waves of fear and anticipation flowing from almost everyone.

He jerked his head up, now wide awake, when the startling news of the Passage Ceremony for Akkal was announced. He clamped down his jealousy with the hue of Mother Sky at dark time as quickly as he could, hoping that pretty Gunda had not received it. Why was this happening? Akkal had not passed the number of summers required, that of all fingers and one foot of toes. He was only two summers older than Jeek.

The mind of Jeek wandered off to his own future Passage Ceremony. He imagined himself standing tall and straight before Hama, taller than he was now, waiting to receive his second name. What would Dakadaga choose for him? What would it be? Jeek the Clever? No, probably not, since Enga Dancing Flower was the only one who called him that. At one time he had desired to be Jeek Beaver Slayer. Most of all, though, he wanted to be Jeek Spear Thrower. He wanted that very badly. He had practiced in secret as often as he could. He did not know how he would practice on the trek, but he would try. He knew well that only females in the Hamapa tribe threw spears. Males, his mother told him often enough, did not have the patience or the skill. Their job was to carve up the meat and drag it back to the village on hides after the females speared the animals.

A gentle thought from Gunda washed over him, bathed in the pink of a private communication. She admonished him for thinking of himself before the tribe. He glanced at her, sending a bashful, drowsy apology, and she smiled at him in a shy way.

Then the second Passage Ceremony, that of Mootak, also was announced. Jeek shook himself even more fully alert, even alarmed. This was serious. Dakadaga must have doubts that either of these two youths would reach fifteen summers. If they did not make it, would any of the tribe survive the coming trek?

He wished both he and pretty Gunda were old enough to dance. After the ceremonies, he watched with admiration as Enga twirled and dipped. Her birth-sister, Ung Strong Arm, danced beside her. Tog and Vala joined in. Bahg Swiftfeet danced with his mate, Fee Long Thrower, while their baby crawled over the stones of their beloved Paved Place. Even old Cabat the Thick moved his feet as quickly as he could.

Jeek felt all the asking pleas being flung to the Spirits. He sent his own upward, concentrating on lifting them all the way to Mother Sky and Dakadaga.

Then Hama did something she rarely did. She flashed a bright red message for all the children to dance as she and her mate, the one she had chosen to be Hapa, the Most High Male, joined in.

Surely, Jeek thought, catching the small, soft hand of Gunda as they stomped around the fire, all the Spirits would hear the Hamapa and their journey would be safe.

Chapter 3

"Neanderthals and Cro-Magnons would have been quite closely related, and genetically there may have been no barrier to Neanderthal/Cro-Magnon interbreeding... Hybrids...may have been discriminated against by the parent populations..."

—*In Search of the Neanderthals,*
Christopher Stringer and Clive Gamble

"Our ancestors likely had sex with Neandertals..."

—from http://news.sciencemag.org/archaeology/
2015/01/humans-and-neandertals-likely-
interbred-middle-east by Michael Balter

Sister Sun was starting to make her climb into Mother Sky when the tribe set out. They had been up and astir for a long time already, assembling their traveling pouches and cutting a few more pieces of mammoth hide. They stripped the hide from the large wipiti of the single males and used it to bundle extra spears and rock tools, along with the dried meat for the journey. At the last moment, Hapa suggested they take the other very large hide also, the one from the wipiti he shared with Hama, and tuck it inside the whole packet to use in case the first one wore out from dragging it for many moons. Panan One Eye argued with Hapa, as he often did, but everyone else could see that it was a good idea and Panan gave up after a short time. Enga Dancing Flower did not know how many moons they would have to travel before they came upon the large herds of mammoth that used to roam in this place. None of them knew that.

Even though the warm season was upon them, the time of new growth, seed season, this early in the day the breath of Mother Sky made its way through their wraps to raise bumps on the skin of their limbs.

Enga took one long last look at the village, the Paved Place that had been built in times past, the Sacred Hill nearby, the places where the wipiti had stood in a semicircle. She paused to listen to the babble of the nearby stream where they had washed their bodies and had gotten their drinking water.

Hama thought-spoke to the whole tribe, *Is everyone ready to depart?*

Many nodded heads and sent back positive vibrations. All except Vala Golden Hair. She approached Enga and Tog Flint Shaper where they stood with their belongings, ready to leave. She carried her baby, Sooka, in a sling on her back. The baby kicked and squirmed, as she often did. Sooka was not content in the sling like most Hamapa babies.

Help me, Tog Flint Shaper, Vala thought-spoke. *I can not get anything done with the baby in my way.*

Enga clenched her teeth. She felt the warmth Tog was sending to Vala. Tog was *her* mate, not that of Vala. Enga stepped forward.

We can help you. She stressed the thought-word "we" with a smile that showed her teeth. *What is it that you cannot do?*

Tog sent Enga a private thought. *You know that her baby is most unruly and hard to manage.*

That was true, Enga had to agree. *But why does she always ask you and no one else?*

Panan One Eye had seen them standing together and came up behind Vala, his eyebrows lowered toward his eyes. Only one of his eyes had sight, the other had been injured during a hunting accident. He had no beard and no hair on his head, but his eyebrows were thick.

Sister Sun glinted her light from his shiny head and also reflected bright rays onto the golden hair of Vala.

What is your problem now, Vala Golden Hair? Enga could feel the irritation in the thought-speak of Panan. It was not directed solely toward Vala. It was sent so that she and Tog could also understand that he was impatient with her.

Vala took her baby from the sling and jiggled her on her hip. *It is Sooka. She has been fussing for a long time now. She did not sleep in the dark time and she is not happy.*

Panan asked, *Why have you waited until it is time to depart to ask for help? I have been ready for a long time. So has Sannum Straight Hair and Cabat the Thick. We could have helped you.*

Enga caught a shred of the private thought from Vala, not cloaked carefully enough.

None of you are as young and strong as Tog Flint Shaper. Those other two are old.

Panan had caught the stray thought also. He grabbed her arm and pulled her toward her pile of belongings, not yet wrapped and ready to drag. He sent an appeal to the other two he had mentioned and Sannum and Cabat both came and made quick work of tying up her bundle.

You must not cause dissension. Most of all, not at this time. The thought-speak of Panan was meant to shame her in front of the tribe, but Vala tossed her long hair, the color of Brother Moon when at his most pale. It fell in smooth waves onto her shoulders.

Enga thought, with some shock, that Vala Golden Hair did not care about the tribe at this moment. She did not always think like a Hamapa. Maybe that was what had made it more easy for her to mate with Stitcher, the outsider. The stomach of Enga had roiled at the thought when Stitcher had made it known to her that he wanted to mate with Enga. She had made sure that did not happen.

Hama spoke privately with Panan One Eye. They did not keep their discussion entirely private and Enga could tell that Hama blamed Panan for some amount of tension in caring for Vala.

Panan argued that Vala had no one to help her, but Hama insisted she had the whole tribe.

Panan had been one of the mates of the Aja Hama when she was the leader of the tribe, so he had been Hapa, the Most High Male. Aja Hama was the name that had been given to the Hama they had all loved so much. She had been called that only after she died. She was their leader for many, many summers. The words "Aja Hama" only meant "Former Most High Female," but they were used to bestow honor on the memory of her. All the Hamapa had mourned her for a long time.

Enga wondered how much Panan missed being Hapa, Most High Male, and having more ranking than he now had. Maybe that was why he disagreed often with Hapa, the mate of Hama. He and Aja Hama had been the birth-parents of Lakala Rippling Water, Fee Long Thrower, and also Tog Flint Shaper. The two had been good leaders. But the ones who were Hama and Hapa now were also good leaders. At least, Enga hoped they were. They had to be good enough to lead the tribe to a new land where they could live and not starve.

At last, the small band set out. Several males took turns dragging the bundle of Vala, along with their own, while she juggled Sooka either on her back or in her arms.

They covered a good amount of distance over the rolling terrain. In low places where Sister Sun did not reach, Brother Earth was still spotted with small patches of the cold white flakes Mother Sky had sent during the Cold Season.

The tribe soon fell into a rhythm. It seemed to Enga that they were making good progress. The individual bundles were not large and not heavy. The most strong males worked with the older males, in pairs, hauling the large pack. Hapa, who had been named Donik Tree Trunk for his large, thick stature, before he was Hapa, was also the most tall male. He worked first with Sannum Straight Hair. Sannum, though he had thirty-six summers, more than twice the seventeen that Enga had passed, had more than enough strength to pull his share. After Sister Sun had traveled four hand lengths, climbing through Mother Sky, Hama called a halt to rest. They laid down their bundles, squatted, and sipped from their water gourds sparingly. They had not encountered any streams and no one knew how much farther they would walk before finding one. They were not going the direction they used to go for hunting, so this land was unfamiliar.

After the stop for rest, Bahg Swiftfeet and Cabat the Thick paired up to drag the heavy pack. Cabat had a slow stride and Bahg was very fast, so they were awkward together. Soon Teek Bearclaw, the birth-brother of Jeek and a strong young male, took the place of Cabat.

Tog and Enga walked side by side. He occasionally took her bundle from her and gave her some relief. That made her smile inside and out. He was concerned for the seed growing within her. He did not glance at Vala Golden Hair, who mostly stayed behind them with Panan One Eye. Their shoulders sometimes rubbed together and Enga felt the warmth of his touch long after they separated.

When Sister Sun had hidden half her face and was beginning to send streaks of color across her Mother Sky, Hama halted once more. She had picked the place wisely. There was a small stream nearby. She pointed to the water and everyone dropped their bundles with eagerness and knelt by the stream to drink.

Enga listened to the noisy lapping, but could also hear rumbling inside her. She was hungry from walking all day, from carrying the seed of Tog inside her as well as her bundle of belongings.

They all knew that their meal would consist of the dried jerky they had carried. No one would have the energy nor the time to seek and kill fresh meat, prepare it, and cook it.

After they ate, everyone looked to Hama expectantly. They did not know what rituals should be followed in this unusual time.

She sent a thought-speak to all of them. *There will be no Saga tonight. We are all tired and must rest for the continuing trek. Perhaps, another time, we will stay in one place for a few days and have music and Saga.*

Hama had indeed chosen the place well. Enga had a fleeting thought that it would be pleasant to dwell here. However, there were no mammoth to be seen or smelled. There were enough tall needled trees to shelter them for dark time. They sat and gnawed on the jerky, each one trying not to eat too much, so it would last as long as possible.

They got their sleeping furs from their bundles. Enga and Tog shared one since they were mates. She was glad that the growing seed had not made her too large to enjoy her mate yet. She knew it happened sometimes.

Ung Strong Arm and Lakala Rippling Water approached.

May we spread our sleeping fur next to yours? Ung asked her birth-sister.

Enga was pleased to have them near. She had been happy when Ung and Lakala had started dwelling in the same wipiti. Ung was the best hunter and Lakala the best singer. It was fitting that two such females should be together.

As she eased herself onto her sleeping skin, Enga noticed that Vala spread her own fur next to that of Panan, but that they did not share one. Perhaps he did not want to be too near the restless baby, who would probably interrupt his sleep.

Enga thought about the amount of jerky in their pouches. It should be enough to get them through the Warm Season, in normal times. Would they all want to eat more when they walked all day? Would they run out of it?

Then, for some reason, she thought about all the tribe members they had lost recently, during the last Cold Season. The last two Hamas had been slain. The tribe nearly fell apart when that happened. Two youths had also been lost, both banished. Kokat No Ear had died on a hunting trip, gored by a peccary. Maybe it was good the tribe was fewer in numbers. Maybe, with less of them, the dried meat would be enough for those on the trek and would last them until they found the place where the game had gone.

There were no sounds of night creatures, no night birds singing. They had fled the Great Ice that destroyed everything in its path.

They were still in the area where the icy blast could be felt when the breath of Mother Sky came from that direction, so many creatures had fled, not just the Hamapa.

She looked up at Mother Sky, gazing down on them with so many twinkling eyes. Enga found the Guiding Bear. At least it was still with them. It had served them well on long distance hunts and on visits to other tribes in the past, but now she did not know where they were going, so maybe it would not always be seen and could not help them.

They were following the trail of the vanished small horses, but who knew where that trail would lead? Enga knew that Hama did not know where they would end up.

Chapter 4

Very early, before Sister Sun appeared, when Mother Sky was taking on the barest of light-hued tints, Hama sent out a picture of the tribe trudging on. Jeek sat up, rubbing his eyes. When he had gotten all the grit out, he reached behind him and rubbed the sore spot on his back from the lump he had slept upon. Closing his eyes again, he brought up the thought of the wipiti he had shared his whole life with his birth-brother, Teek Bearclaw, and his mother, Zhoo of Still Waters, the Healer of the tribe. Their father, Mahk Long Eye, had died many seasons ago.

But that wipiti did not now stand. A new one would stand in the new village. It was that thought that got him up and going.

Everyone arose and packed up the sleeping furs. They grabbed a few quick bites, filled their water gourds, and started off.

The second day was very much like the first. They encountered no more streams. They smelled no more game. Sister Sun wrapped herself in thick cloud garments and Mother Sky blew cold breath across the barren land. *Why was her breath so cold at this time?* Jeek shivered. It should be getting warmer.

Hama overheard his thoughts and answered, *We must travel far to get to a place where Mother Sky will be kinder with her breath, where Sister Sun will want to show her face.*

It wasn't long, only a journey the length of one hand for Sister Sun, before Mother Sky started shedding frigid tears, soaking everyone and everything that they wore. The animal hides would protect the things wrapped in them, but the skin of Brother Earth got softer and softer until each foot was coated in heavy mud.

Jeek, go to that rise. He looked in the direction that the thought-speak had come from. Hama nodded at him and pointed to a small high place not far away. *See if there is any shelter in sight.*

Eager to help, Jeek handed his pack to his birth-brother, Teek Bearclaw, and ran like the quickest gust from Mother Sky to the knoll. He scrambled to the top and surveyed the land. Endless rolling plains stretched out before him. He turned in every direction and, at last, spotted something different. They were not trees. They were people. Two tall males, loping across the ground toward them. Jeek waved his arms to hail them and they waved back.

He sent the picture back to Hama, adding the thought that maybe they would know this land and would be able to tell the Hamapa where to go. He did not get a return thought, but felt a stir of caution.

Stay there until they are more near to you, she thought-spoke to him. *But come back with speed and join us before they reach you.*

To Jeek, the two looked like Hamapa, sturdy people with strong limbs. They drew closer and he studied them. One had hair the color of fire, like many Hamapa, braided with leather strips. The other, a bit more tall, had hair the color of dark mud, done in a top knot with, he thought as he squinted, a bone through it, much like Tog Flint Shaper, whose hair was held by a bone Enga Dancing Flower had carved for him.

They wore fur capes similar to the ones the Hamapa wore. Jeek hoped they were enough like them that all could understand each other. If they were a different kind of people, it would be difficult to communicate, since thought-speak would not get through to them.

He sent back to Hama a picture of what he was seeing. When the two got close enough that he could clearly see their eyes, he scurried down the hill and rejoined his people.

The two males slowed as they approached the tribe. The brothers and sisters stood still, waiting for the strangers to reach them. It had happened in the past that strangers had meant harm. That was rare, but it was best, Jeek knew, to be cautious. He noticed that the females did not hold their spears, but stood near them. Some of the males would have chopping stones in pouches that could be extracted in a flash. The direct gaze of the wise Hama did not waver until the pair stood before her.

Do you understand this thought? Hama directed this to the males, but in such a way that the tribe standing close behind her could also receive the message.

The male with the fire-colored hair moved only his head, to look at his partner. They exchanged private thoughts. Then the one with mud-colored hair, who was taller, answered. *We do understand. We are Gata. Do you know the Gata?*

There was a stirring in the tribe. They all knew of the Gata. They had been a tribe who dwelt not far from the Hamapa, people they had traded with. As the last Cold Season had approached, the Gata leader had sent a message in thought-speak to Hama and had asked if they could take any of them in as they did not have enough food for the whole tribe. She had been forced to tell them that her people did not have any to spare. Part of that tribe had traveled far away to try to start a new tribe.

Jeek could hear Hama going over these details in her mind. So could the two Gata males.

We are Hamapa, Hama answered.

We are from the Gata remnant who left.

You lived through the Cold Season, Hama returned.

We did. But most did not. We and one female are all that are left. We are looking for that female. She went to find game many suns ago and has not returned.

Hama puzzled this, drawing her brows down. *Why has she not returned? Have you had no thoughts from her?*

We have not.

Jeek wondered if the female was alive. What could keep her from communicating with her two tribe mates? Maybe she was hurt, but why would she not send back her thoughts? He looked around at the unfamiliar feature-less land. She could be lost. But again, what would keep her from sending back her thoughts?

The one with the mud-colored hair fell to his knees. His eyes closed and his head drooped. Hapa, the Most High Male, stepped to his side and took his hand. *Are you not well?*

That was when Jeek noticed how thin they both were. It was hard to see what shape their bodies were in beneath their heavy capes, but their cheeks were sunken and their hands scrawny, like bird talons.

Hama and Hapa must have noticed that also, because they each took a piece of jerky from their pack and handed it to the Gata males.

I am Hama of the Hamapa, she thought-spoke as she watched them devour the dried strips.

I am Bodd Blow Striker. That was the one with hair of fire. He drew a cutting stone from his pouch to show them his work.

The other one, still on his knees, also gave his name. *I am called Fall Cape Maker. But I have not made a cape in many moon cycles.*

Bodd explained. *There was game here when we first came. Not much, but some. We have not seen any in too long a time now.*

Hapa and Hama motioned for the whole tribe to be seated for an impromptu council.

They walked away from the newcomers before sitting to fling thoughts back and forth. Hama wanted to take the strangers in but some did not. Enga Dancing Flower and Ung Strong Arm, of course, voted to let them in, since they had been adopted by the tribe as very young children after their own tribe had abandoned them. Tog Flint Shaper did not want them to join the band and to take food from his mate, afraid of damage to his seed growing within her. Vala Golden Hair was also concerned about her infant, she thought-spoke. Panan voted against letting them come along, but Jeek thought that might have been because he usually opposed the vote of Hapa.

Most of the time, the tribe eventually reached a unanimous decision, but this time Hama overruled the dissenters without much discussion. Maybe she thought it would take too long for everyone to agree. Or maybe she thought they would never all agree.

Hama rose, shaking her dark hair and rattling the shells in her braids. Her coloring was as dark as that of her birth-sister, Vala Golden Hair, was light. She approached Bodd and Fall and welcomed them to travel with the Hamapa if they wished.

We do wish to do that. We also wish to look for our female along the way.

Hama agreed that they would all keep watch for her. Bodd and Fall seemed much renewed after eating, and they all continued on their way, searching for the missing female.

* * *

It was several suns after Bodd Blow Striker and Fall Cape Maker had joined the tribe. Enga Dancing Flower had held some anger toward her mate for his unkindness regarding them for some time, but she was no longer angry. He had made her understand, in thoughts and in caresses, that he had been considering her own well being.

Just before the time of darkness fell, as most of them were preparing to have something to eat before they slept, two of the Hamapa males and one female ventured off to look for game. Sannum Straight Hair, one of the older males, and Teek Bearclaw set off at a lope, following a set of paw prints in the soft dirt. They both thought the tracks had been made by caribou. If they found a caribou, Fee Long Thrower, who was with them, carried her spear in readiness to bring it down.

Enga gnawed a piece of jerky. She watched Whim, the baby of Fee and Bahg, crawling in the dirt, getting chewed bits of jerky from the adults. He had been given the name Whim in the early Naming Ceremony, held before they left. It would have been nice to have the ceremony in the new place, and after Whim and Sooka had been alive for twenty full moon cycles, the number of all fingers and all toes. That was the way it had always been done.

She tried to imagine their new place. It could not be in these barren lands. They had to find a place with much water and plant growth, to support the large animals they must have for food, clothing, and tools.

She was getting weary of having nothing but hard, dried meat to eat. The tribe had survived on jerky during many Cold Seasons, but was accustomed to having fresh meat in the warm and hot seasons.

However, she tamped down her annoyance and impatience. She knew that they must make this trek to survive. They could not have stayed where they were. The Great Ice was approaching and the winds that swept off it were so cold, many things died as it approached, plants and animals alike. If they kept going, they would escape the area of blight created by the ice. Hama had told them that Dakadaga promised that. They would get to the land Enga dreamed about. She put her hand inside her waist pouch and rubbed the wooden figure of Aja Hama, who had been so dear to her. Maybe it was not a proper thing to do, but she sent pleas for well-being out to the spirit of the Aja Hama. She was not an actual Spirit, the kind they danced and sang to, but Enga did not care. She petitioned her anyway.

She heard shouting. Sannum and Teek and Fee were back very quickly. Had they found game? Would they eat fresh flesh?

The tribe surged toward the returning ones, hope in every heart. However, the hands of both Sannum and Teek were empty. Fee dragged her spear behind, her head was bowed.

Teek closed his eyes and gave out a picture of what they had seen.

Enga drew in her breath when she saw the form of a female, torn apart.

The cat of long tooth, Ung thought-spoke.

Others agreed. The female had encountered a cat and the cat had slain her.

Bodd and Fall, in spite of being still somewhat weak, followed Teek at a quick pace back to where they had found the body, beside a tiny brackish pool.

When they returned, they both shed tears. Their shoulders shook.

She was my mate, thought-spoke Bodd. *We have lost two babies. And now I have lost her.*

Enga felt her own tears forming and her lips trembled. What a horrible thing to happen after losing two babies, which was a horrible thing already.

Vala Golden Hair stepped forward and put a hand on his shoulder to comfort him.

There was discussion of what to do, whether or not they should spend the time and energy on a proper funeral. The Gata males told them that their own funerals were similar to those of the Hamapa.

Thoughts were exchanged as they squatted together to eat and sip small amounts of water. At last it was decided by all, even Bodd, that they should proceed. They would leave her body for the animals and it would return to Brother Earth.

Before everyone lay down to sleep, Hama asked Bodd what his mate had been called.

She was Gung. Gung Lion Slayer.

Hama jerked upright.

She kept her thought private, but Enga knew what she was thinking. The name of Hama had been Roh Lion Hunter before she was elected Hama. This Gung Lion Slayer of the Gata must have slain a lion, as Hama had. She must have been brave and strong. She had been in a weakened state to have been slain by the large cat now. Enga shook her head. Yes, the Gata female had been hungry. The males were, so she would have been also.

Enga was able to perceive the mourning of Bodd and Fall as their heavy grief stirred the air about them, washing over all the Hamapa also.

As Enga fell asleep, she put her hand on the strong shoulder of Tog, gladdened that they were both alive and that their baby, still a seed, would have a better chance than the babies of Gung and Bodd. Tog laid his warm hand atop the place where their seed grew. Her tears fell once more.

Chapter 5

Yellow-cheeked vole, *Microtus xanthognathus*

"The yellow-cheeked vole, or taiga vole, is an extant species of rodent that is currently found in central Alaska and northwestern Canada. As with many other rodents, this species serves as a good proxy indicator of local paleoenvironmental conditions, and its presence in Wisconsinan-aged deposits in the Midwestern U.S. indicates that regional temperatures were much cooler during this period."

> — from http://iceage.museum.state.il.us/
> mammals/yellow-cheeked-vole-0

Heather vole, *Phenacomys intermedius*

Phenacomys intermedius…is a small, mouse-like rodent with short tail, large hindfeet, and small ears and eyes. They have long, soft brown to grayish fur, with white to pale gray face and feet, and a silvery belly.

> — from http://iceage.museum.state.il.us/
> mammals/heather-vole-0

When they had been travelling for several more suns, as the tribe stopped early, before dark time, Jeek asked Gunda if she would loan him her spear. Hamapa males did not throw spears, but Jeek had always wanted to be a spear thrower and to bring down food for his tribe. Back in the village, he had practiced in secret until he was able to cast his crude spear long and straight. When he was found out, the females let him practice with them. He had not thrown a spear for many suns. He was afraid he would forget his skills.

Ongu Small One heard Jeek and Gunda and approached them. *I have an extra spear, Jeek. Do you want to use it for practice? It would be good if some of the young ones practiced.*

He was pleased because he had not brought one with him.

He and Gunda hurried away from the tribe so they would be able to practice while there was still some light. The place Hama had chosen for their stop was one without shelter or water. Jeek and Gunda walked across flat, dusty land, looking for something they could aim at, but they could find nothing.

We will have to set something up for a target, Gunda thought-spoke.

How will we do that? All that is here is grass—tall grass, but sparse.

That is true. Even if we make a target, we would have to clear the grasses out of the way so we could shoot at it.

The grass was taller than the two young ones. In places it was sparse, but in other places dense. Small creatures scurried through the growth, unseen.

If there was a large animal, we could spear it and eat it, Jeek thought-spoke.

If there was a large animal, we could not see it in this tall grass. Let us be still and see if one of the small animals will appear. We could spear it. If it is good to eat, we can take it back. If it is not, that will be our practice.

They crouched next to each other and listened to the busy animals. They smelled like rodents, which were sometimes good to eat, but usually small. One small vole, with fur the color of the dirt, peeked through the stems at them. Jeek reached for his spear with as much quietness and slowness as he could. The tiny black eyes followed the movement of his hand. When he had picked up the spear, he realized the vole was probably too close for throwing, but maybe he could stab it. As he drew his arm back, the vole scampered off and disappeared. They could track the progress of the vole as the grasses swayed and swished in a zig-zag pattern.

Jeek and Gunda both laughed. Jeek shielded his thought that he did not care if he practiced, or if they hit anything. Being alone with Gunda was a joy for him.

They sat together, not communicating anything, listening to the drone and buzz of insects, the rustling of animals passing them by, and soaking in the heat and the smells.

In all of his memory, Jeek had liked Gunda. In more recent times he had daydreamed about mating with her, giving her his seed, and having babies together. Pretty Gunda, with eyes the color of spring leaves and thick hair like a waterfall of fire. She was often in his dreams as he slept. She had passed eleven summers and Jeek had passed twelve. Before too many more, it would be possible for them to mate. They would never have a First Coupling in the Holy Cave, though. It had been left behind. But he envisioned a new Holy Cave in the place they were going to. It looked much like the old Holy Cave in his mind.

Gradually, Jeek realized that someone was near. He smelled them first, then heard them. The newcomers were not being quiet and must have not been alert to the smell of Gunda and Jeek. The slight breeze blew from the new ones toward them. The almost still air did not send enough scent to tell who approached. The two young ones both stayed motionless, not knowing who was coming.

When Jeek heard a female laughing, he knew who it was, Vala Golden Hair.

Gunda sent a private message. *It is Vala Golden Hair and she is with a male.*

What male do you think she is with?

Panan One Eye?

Tog Flint Shaper?

They were both wrong. Vala and the male lay in the grass not far from them and began to couple. When they were done, Gunda and Jeek were both able to receive their unshielded thoughts. The male was Bodd Blow Striker. He told Vala about his skill at making stone tools. He said he had been the best of the Gata tribe.

Gunda sent another private thought. *How would we ever know if he was the best or not? The rest of the Gata are gone. I think he is bragging.*

Jeek stifled a giggle, as did Gunda. *We could ask his tribe-brother, Fall Cape Maker.*

That made Gunda giggle so hard she snorted out of her nose just a bit.

Someone is here, thought-spoke Bodd with alarm.

Why do you care? asked Vala.

I care because it is too soon to couple with another. Gung Lion Slayer has just died. I should be grieving for a time.

I am helping you grieve.

Jeek and Gunda almost giggled aloud again.

We are leaving now. They heard Bodd straightening his garments and walking away. Angry waves came from Vala, but she soon followed him.

The two young ones felt they should stay where they were for a long time. Vala and Bodd had not known who was listening to them and they did not want them to ever know. It grew dark. They were not sure which way to go, since all they could see was tall grass.

I will have my brother, Teek Bearclaw, show us the way, Jeek thought-spoke. *He will be careful and not let anyone know we are out here.* He sent a message to Teek, who responded immediately. Teek walked into the grass and made a noise like an owl, since it was dark time and owls would be flying now. They jumped up and ran toward his sound, relieved.

Chapter 6

"Humans first reached Flores [a small Indonesian island] when the sea level was exceptionally low, and the island was easily accessible from the mainland. When the seas rose again, some people were trapped on the island, which was poor in resources. Big people, who need a lot of food, died first. Smaller fellows survived much better. Over the generations, the people of Flores became dwarves. This unique species, known by scientists as *Homo floresiensis*, reached a maximum height of only one metre and weighed no more than twenty-five kilograms. [Author: 3.28 feet, 55.1 pounds] They were nevertheless able to produce stone tools, and even managed occasionally to hunt down some of the island's elephants—though, to be fair, the elephants were a dwarf species as well."

> —*Sapiens, A Brief History of Humankind*,
> Yuval Noah Harari, p.7

From where she squatted, her arms resting on her knees, Enga Dancing Flower tipped her face up and watched Brother Moon make his way across the darkened surface of Mother Sky. He wore wisps of gray clothing, but his round face shone through brightly. The Hamapa had been traveling for one moon cycle, from round face to round face of Brother Moon. How many cycles would it take, Enga wondered, before they found a land like theirs had been before the Great Ice approached? She missed the land of the old Sagas, where everyone had plenty to eat and everyone had extra garments, not only for warmth, but also for special ceremonies. The nights had not been as warm as they should be during this warm season, and Enga had begun wearing her bear skin cape, the cape she usually saved for dancing. Her everyday mammoth skin wrap showed signs of wear and did not keep the cold wind from her skin. Soon she would need a new one.

Hama had told them they were to stay in this place for two suns and rest. Everyone was weary of walking all day, every day, for so long. Enga looked forward to hearing a song and a Saga. From the buzzing of thoughts in the air, everyone else anticipated this with pleasure also.

Despite the small, stocky stature of Hama, she always presented an air of command. Her birth-mother had been a Hama, but Enga did not think that was what gave her the natural authority she had. She had borne three daughters who lived, and also one more child, who was born dead. But before all of that she had slain a mighty lion by herself. She was still strong. Now, when she drew herself to her full height and the rest of the Hamapa sat looking up to her, she seemed taller than she was. Her dark, bright eyes flashed, catching a strong beam from Brother Moon, almost as they had before the trek started and everyone had grown so weary. Hama nodded to the Singer, Lakala Rippling Water.

They had no central blazing fire, no place of paved stones, but they were gathered in a circle as if those things were there. Tog Flint Shaper took his place next to Enga, but Vala Golden Hair edged in next to him on the other side. The mate she had been traveling with for the last several suns, Panan One Eye, was beside Hama so that he could give the Saga after Lakala sang.

Lakala Rippling Water stood and lifted her eyes to Brother Moon, who smiled upon her and bathed her in his light, briefly, before a thick, dark gray piece of his clothing drifted across his face. She was tall, as her birth-mother had been. Lakala had been born of Aja Hama, the one Enga revered and whose image she carried. Aja Hama had also birthed Fee Long Thrower and Tog Flint Shaper, making her all the more beloved by Enga.

Lakala started a slow Song of Blessing to Dakadaga, the Spirit of Mother Sky, then trilled a more energetic plea to the Spirit of the Hunt. Her pure tones seemed to still the sounds of the insects.

Surely the Spirits would smile on their trek and bring them safely to a new land. How could they resist the beautiful music, Enga wondered.

As Lakala sat, Panan, the Storyteller, rose. He started the Saga of the Little People, the ones the Hamapa called Mikino. Several interjected with a question about why he chose that Saga.

Are we near the place where the Mikino live?

If we are near them, will this Saga draw them to us?

Even though the Mikino were short, dark people with small heads on their tiny, sharp shoulders, the Hamapa feared them. They were fierce fighters and befriended no one. The Hamapa had traded with them, but were cautious always when they dealt with the slender, delicate-looking people.

Panan lifted his shoulders together with his thick eyebrows in answer. Brother Moon shone off his bald pate and, to Enga, lent him an extra air of authority. Panan said he did not know why he chose this Saga, but he continued. He told how the Mikino ate much less meat than the Hamapa, enjoying grains and plants. A shudder went around the group at this. Some pursed their lips as if they had a bad taste in their mouths. They would eat plants when they had to, but did not like them. The Hamapa would eat only meat whenever they could. It was how it had always been.

The Mikino kept large cats captive and had traded their beautiful pelts when they got low on meat while the Hamapa had plenty. In spite of having the thick furs to trade, they themselves wore thin animal skins, usually horse hides that were untreated and crude.

Panan sent a picture of a Mikino village that he had gotten from the Storyteller before him, and that Storyteller had gotten from the one before him, back into the time when one Hamapa had been to the place and saved the mental picture. The Hamapa had all seen this picture through Panan many times, but none living now had ever been inside one of their villages.

Their shacks were crude and made with sticks and grasses and smelled of the bodies of the filthy Mikino. The shacks were not like sturdy Hamapa wipitis, when they had been set up in a permanent place, weighted with stones and held up with solid mammoth tusks. Just outside the Mikino village there were caves. The Storyteller let them hear a mighty roar, then took them to the caves where the jaguars were kept. The small beings made the barriers much sturdier than their own dwellings, piling up thick logs to block the cave entrances and keep the mighty cats captive. The Hamapa had not ever seen cats that large. The tigers and other cats they encountered were smaller.

The Storyteller showed them a view inside the cave, through a chink in the logs, as it had been seen by the ancient Hamapa visitor. This Saga took place at dark time and, in the thought-pictures, Brother Moon sent a beam into the cave through a gap at the top. They got a glimpse of large cats, jaguars, their coats of the most light brown shade, and spotted with dark black and brown butterfly-shaped spots. One animal turned its head and stared at them with glowing, golden eyes. Everything else was in darkness, for the Mikino used no fire and ate their food uncooked. They fed their enemies to the cats. It was also said that they ate their own babies.

Many Hamapa had suspected the Mikino who lived near their old home when their Aja Hama was slain, had been the ones who killed her.

Enga drew her bear skin close about her neck, yet shivered from thinking about such vicious little beings. She hoped never to see one. She would also never want to meet one of their fearsome jaguars while it was alive. Only if it was dead and she could strip off and scrape the pelt. No Hamapa wore jaguar pelts now, but they used to. She had seen one when she was a small child, and she cast her mind back to that time. She remembered running her fingers along the patterns, not like any other animal she knew.

Tog broke the concentration of Enga. He leaned to Vala and picked up her squirming baby, who was just starting to make irritated noises. Enga scowled and tried to rejoin Panan in the Saga. She was conscious that neither Tog nor Vala were paying attention to it. One other was not attentive to the Saga either. Bodd Blow Striker, the new Gata with red hair, seemed to be concentrating on Vala and Tog. Enga clamped her jealousy as tightly as she could, in her own personal private shade of dark blue.

A hot-colored thought seared through her mind cloak, though, before she could return to the Mikino village with Panan. Mootak Big Heart seethed. His angry thought was clear. He would have chosen a more apt Saga for this night, if only Panan would let him assume the title of Hava, Storyteller.

The old man is too ancient. A younger one, like me, should take over.

Enga shot him a private warning. *Your thoughts are being heard by everyone.* Mootak glanced her way, frightened. She knew he feared being disciplined for his feelings if others heard them. The tribe ignored him, however. Maybe, Enga thought, they were all too weary to bother with the transgression of a young one. Enga was certain it would not happen again. Those thoughts would not be displayed publicly. She knew he would think them, though.

Panan had probably not received the stray thoughts, as he was concentrating on recalling and transmitting the Saga of the Mikino. The Saga ended with the Hamapa male leaving the Mikino village unharmed, and with several jaguar pelts he had received for the pouches of dried mammoth jerky he had taken there to trade. Sounds like high-pitched jeering laughter followed the Hamapa male as he left.

Enga did not want the gathering to end with this. She wanted Lakala to sing again and she wanted to dance. She had not danced enough since they had left the old village. Maybe that was a thought that dwelt on herself too much, but she did think that Dakadaga had always brought good fortune to the tribe, in part, because of the dancing of Enga, the best dancer. When her dances were joined with the flute and the drum, what Spirit could resist?

She wafted a tentative thought to Hama about dancing and more music, but Hama answered that everyone was weary.

When all lay down for sleep, Enga was disturbed by visions of tiny, sharp-toothed beings who wore untanned skins and stank of their own filth. The beings in her vision gobbled up the infant of Vala and even that of Enga, the one that had not yet emerged from her body.

Chapter 7

"Ice Age jaguars...were at least 15 to 20 percent larger than living jaguars (*Panthera onca*)... During the...Wisconsinan ice age (71,000 to 10,000 years ago) the northern boundary of their range stretched from Nevada, Kansas, Mississippi, and Tennessee... Jaguars (were) the largest New World cat and the only one that can roar... (T)hey presumably resembled living jaguars, with beautifully spotted coats distinctly different from the tan coats of lions."

—Ice Age Mammals of North America:
A Guide to the Big, the Hairy, and the Bizarre
by Ian M. Lange, p. 110–111

When Sister Sun had traveled three hand lengths above the surface of Brother Earth, the Hamapa began to feel uneasy. The land here held a few puny plants, but nothing big enough to support large animals. They could not remain here and be inactive. So they gathered their belongings and equipment, and began to move again.

They walked along a row of stunted trees of white bark until they gave way to even more stunted shrub plants. There could not be a danger of a large unnoticed animal in this land. Here, too, was a place the mammoth had fled. But something unknown was unsettling the tribe.

Jeek began to notice that there was a foul odor in the air. Panan eventually held up his hand and halted the tribe. He raised his nose and sniffed. Jeek sniffed deeply, too. The last Saga surged into his mind. This was the odor of the filthy small people. Mikino were near!

Jeek saw Tog Flint Shaper look around, but he was not looking for the little people. He spotted Vala Golden Hair and her awful child and moved to put his arm around her shoulder. Jeek frowned.

This was not right. Tog was the mate of Enga Dancing Flower. They should stay together to protect each other. The older birth-brother of Jeek, Teek Bearclaw, was near to their mother, so Jeek walked to Enga and patted her hand. He was rewarded with a smile, but her eyes darted away from him, watching Tog and Vala. Her eyes were sad.

As Jeek stood next to Enga, his mind was filled with buzzing from the tribe. There was much agitation at the thought that the Mikino were near enough to smell. Jeek sniffed again, very deep into his nose and brain, and almost recoiled at the odor of the little people. This odor had been conveyed to them with the stories of Panan, so they all knew what it was.

A mighty roar split the air. Jaguar! Jeek nearly fell to his knees. The fearsome cats in their cages were near enough to hear. The tribe was very, very close to the Mikino village. The smell of fear sprouted from each Hamapa.

Now Jeek caught a whiff of the large cats. The hair on his skin prickled and rose up.

The tribe had still not reached a place where game abounded, so they all knew the Mikino must be hungry. Even if they ate a large amount of plants, there were not many plants here.

Jeek wondered why they had not left this place, but before he could think further, the small beings burst upon them from the scraggly brush.

Their high-pitched shrieks paralyzed the Hamapa, filled them with terror for a moment. Then each female dropped her pack and reached inside for her spear. Each male drew his knife from his waist pouch.

Before anyone could lay a weapon on a Mikino, they had slid close and cut the food pouches from most of the adults. They were very quick. Fee Long Thrower and Ung Strong Arm, the two best mammoth hunters, flung spears at the thieves as they scurried away. Ung hit one in his tiny leg. All of them raced away. The wounded Mikino left a trail of Red. It was a trail no Hamapa would follow, as it would lead to their village. That was a place they would not go.

Jeek saw Panan sitting and holding his leg. He drew closer and noticed Red gushing from the leg. He called his mother, the Healer, and she dressed the wound with honey and dried grasses, then bound it with a strip of hide.

Hama and Hapa both urged the tribe to get out of the area quickly. All obeyed. Several more roars sounded as they fled.

Vala Golden Hair had seen the injury of Panan and let him lean on her as they went.

When they had marched quickly for as long as they could, dragging their burdens, and those with young carrying them when they could no longer walk, Hapa told them to stop.

We have gone far enough. No one is following us. We must see how much food we have left.

Vala still had her pouch, since Tog had pushed the thieves off her. Hama also had hers. The Elder males and several others had made a barrier around her. But there were only those two pouches of jerky. Cabat the Thick looked upward and shuffled his feet, then thought-spoke to his tribe.

I have some dried fish in my bundle.

Jeek felt the disapproval aimed at Cabat. They all knew he had meant to keep the fish for himself. He would never have shared it if this disaster had not happened. Jeek kept the thought to himself, but he wondered what else could go wrong. Were the Hamapa, the Most High People, beginning to act a bit like the Mikino? Keeping food to oneself was not the Hamapa way. He had thought the troubles within the tribe, the large troubles, were over after the killer of the former Hama was found. He thought his tribe would all see that they had to pull together to make it to a land where they could live. If they did not pull together, they might not make it there.

An even darker thought came from Hama.

We have traveled in the wrong direction, fleeing the small people. We are going toward the Great Ice. We must keep going away from it.

The three Elders, Hama, Hapa, and Panan conferred together after Vala helped Panan to sit by the other two.

The rest squatted and caught their breath.

* * *

Enga Dancing Flower was hungry. She wondered if she was hungry only in her mind, because she knew how little food they had, or if she was truly hungry from the fast pace they had kept up for half a day. She knew, as did all of the tribe, that she needed to eat an extra amount to feed the growing baby inside her. Enga was the only female carrying a baby. That would not be a good thing for the tribe if they were settled. That was because the tribe needed always to have more babies. Members were often lost. The Hamapa were sometimes slain during the hunt, sometimes fell ill and did not recover, and sometimes had other accidents. To replace those who were lost, more needed to be born. On the trek, however, having only one pregnant female was easier.

Now she felt pains. Were they in her stomach? Or were they in the sac of the baby? She wrapped her arms around her knees as she squatted, and held tight, her fingers squeezing the color out of her knuckles.

Tog came up behind her and put his strong fingers on her shoulders. He rubbed them and she felt her shoulders lower and her mind relax. She uncurled her fingers and flexed them.

He sat behind her and she leaned against his broad, solid chest. She moved only her eyes to see that Panan One Eye had returned to the side of Vala and was tossing Sooka in the air to amuse her.

Are you in pain? Tog asked. *I felt your aching just now.*

I was, Enga answered. *But my distress is easing. I think I am just hungry. But we will all be hungry before we reach the end of this journey. I must not complain, but must learn to accept these feelings.*

I will give you part of my share of the jerky when we stop for the night.

That was as it should be, but she was glad he was doing the right thing.

At last, the Elders nodded at each other and stood to listen to Hama address the tribe.

Hama held her arms high and turned her face up to Mother Sky.

The tribe stirred. She was going to give them a Pronouncement.

"Hoody!" she spoke aloud. The tribe heard the word, *Listen!* They obeyed.

"Yaya, Hama vav."

Yes, the Most High Female speaks.

"Hamamapapa nasa ba wa Mikino. Hamamapapa poos wa Dakadaga kal dy."

The Hamapa cannot stay near the Mikino. The Hamapa must go where the Spirit of Mother Sky goes to sleep each day.

She closed as she always did.

"Dakadaga sheesh Hamamapapa."

The Spirit of Mother Sky, bless the Hamapa.

Hama raised one arm slowly in a great arc, indicating that they must make a journey in a large circle that took them far from the Mikino. Only then would they be able to move in the direction they must go. Some more progress was made before they stopped for sleeping. A few of the remaining pieces of jerky were passed around and each person took one bite. Tog made Enga take two. She could have eaten many pieces. Her stomach made noises like an animal.

Chapter 8

The flat land was endless. It was the same every day. For all of her life before this trek, Enga Dancing Flower had rejoiced when she saw Sister Sun appearing after dark time. A new day had meant good things then. It had meant being safe with her tribe, being with her birth-sister, being near Tog Flint Shaper—and getting closer and closer to him. Every new sun was cause for joy.

Now she groaned when a new sun appeared above the rim of Brother Earth. It meant another long walk across land that looked exactly like all the other land. Another dark time in a place that looked just like the last one. The only differences were that sometimes there was a bit of water, a trickle from a stream. Some of the water they found was still and tasted sour. When there was no water, they were careful to sip slowly out of the gourds they carried.

What if this land never ended? Could it go on and never stop, never change?

Everyone was so tired. They got more hungry every day.

Fee Long Thrower speared a small rabbit one day and Sannum Straight Hair managed to trap three tiny voles once, but they were eaten uncooked, as the savage Mikino ate their food. Hama told them they had to protect the fire they carried. Akkal Firetender was doing a good job keeping the smoldering embers in his horn from going out. She did not want to disturb his good work.

At the next new sun, Enga bent her sore legs and looked at the bottoms of her feet before she rose. They were raw and cracked. The tribe no longer had enough skins to wrap the feet of everyone. The remaining foot skins went to the Elders. Their feet were older and more tender. The leg of Panan had healed after Vala Golden Hair had helped him walk for several days, but he still limped.

How could any of them walk one more sun?

When Enga surveyed the surroundings, she knew they could not stay here, either. There was nothing for them in this place. They had to walk.

Tog waved his arms at her. *Look. In the far distance.* Tog put his hands on her head and turned it in the direction he was looking. *Do you see it?*

She did. Her smile broke through her gloom. *The land is different. There are hills.*

Finally, they would be off this plain, so barren, so devoid of life. The slight rolling hills looked far, but they would have to make it there. Enga rubbed the smooth, wooden tummy of the Aja Hama. She drew it from her pouch and showed it to Tog.

His eyes grew wide. The Aja Hama had been his birth-mother and he recognized it immediately.

You still have this carving? You have kept it all this time?

She leaned close to him. *She has gotten us this far. Her spirit is with us. She is guiding us.*

Tog mumbled something about guiding them to the Mikino, but he patted her arm and continued packing up with a smile on his broad face.

It was three more suns before they drew near the hills. If they had been stronger, that might have been only two. They were all so weakened and moving so much more slowly than normal. However, when they could smell the verdant trees on the hills, the pace quickened. Enga could see faint smiles on many faces. She studied her tribe mates as they stepped up their pace.

Bodd Blow Striker, the shorter red-haired Gata male, had carried the baby of Vala Golden Hair for the last two suns. But Enga saw the way Vala looked at Panan One Eye. Panan had left her side after he could walk unaided. Now Vala was trying to make Panan jealous and was trying to win him back. At least she was not going near Tog. That was a relief to Enga.

From so many rough days, dissentions had sprung up. Hapa had always resented the fact the Panan had not supported his mate in the last election for Hama. She had been chosen by the rest of the tribe in spite of that, but sometimes it seemed that Panan still opposed Hama and Hapa for no good reason.

Mootak Big Heart also aimed ill will toward Panan at times. Especially when Panan gave the Saga and Mootak could have given it as well. During the first part of the trek, Mootak sat for lessons from Panan, as he had done for many seasons before they left. Enga did not think he was doing this now.

Hapa had even been heard telling some of the tribe that it would be better when Mootak took over the Saga from Panan and when Panan retired from any leadership in the tribe. Hama did nothing to stop her mate from spreading his opinions. Enga did not think that was right. Enga pondered how so much discord swirled around Panan One Eye.

As soon as they reached a place with animals to eat, they would all behave as Hamapa should behave. Full bellies would help everything look better. Enga sent a plea to Dakadaga for that time to come soon. She had begun to wonder if Dakadaga was receiving the thoughts that the Hamapa sent to her.

Chapter 9

"Scientists have reconstructed the whole…genome of a group of ancient humans called Denisovans. …(T)hey had dark hair, eyes, and skin, the journal Science reports."

—*UK Natural History Museum online* (http://www.nhm.ac.uk/about-us/news/2012/august/denisovan-dna-suggests-a-dark-complexion-and-interbreeding113697.html) 31 August 2012

At last they were close enough to see the trees clearly. Jeek was a little disappointed that they were so small, but any trees were better than the endless plain they had been across. He blinked when he realized that there were beings standing in the trees, watching them approach. Some were almost taller than the scrubby growth. They were all taller than the Hamapas. But they did not look like the Tall Ones that he had known. Some of the brothers and sisters of Jeek had dark hair and dark eyes, but these new people were like none he had ever seen, with hair, eyes, and skin darker than a night when Brother Moon stays away and cloud garments hide the many eyes of Mother Sky.

The dark ones watched the tired band approach, not moving, not speaking. They were so different, they would probably not understand any Hamapa words or thoughts, Jeek thought.

Hama raised her hand for them to stop at the foot of a hill. The strangers stood slightly above them on the side of the small rise.

Hama sent a greeting to them with thought-speak. Jeek knew it would not work, but it was good to try, to be certain. Next, Hama tried loud speech.

"Vishoo?" Hama asked. That meant *hill people.*

"Hoo hoo," one of them answered.

"Hoo hoo hoo," echoed the rest.

Hama pointed to her group. "Hoody. Hamamapapa," telling them to listen, these were the Hamapa people.

Several of the tall dark strangers took up the chant, "Hoody, hoody, hoody."

Vala Golden Hair, who had been lagging behind, caught up to the group. Bodd Blow Striker had walked with her and carried the baby. Jeek thought she looked more pale than she usually did. She staggered forward to the front of the group, held her hands out to the strangers, and fell to her knees. Then she pitched forward onto her face before anyone could grab her. Her hair flowed around her face and onto the dirt like a golden river.

Panan and Tog started forward, and Bodd reached out with the arm not carrying Sooka, but one of the strangers darted down the hill and got to her first. "Woo woo? Moo moo?" he asked. Without waiting for answers to his incomprehensible questions, he gestured to one of his companions. One other came forward with a skin sac of water, and held it to her lips.

When Vala had revived enough to stand and walk, she and the exhausted band followed the strangers to their village. Bodd stayed close to Vala.

Jeek could see that these people were friendly, so far, but would they stay that way? How could anyone tell if they would or not? Were they luring them to the village to eat them? He was almost to the point that he would have gone along with that. He couldn't go much farther without more to eat. None of them could.

Jeek was cheered when he smelled smoke, then saw the ashes of a fire. Fire meant food—he hoped. Beyond the firepit were some huts, but they were not proper houses. Instead, they were made of large pieces of a skin he had never seen, and were propped up with poles of tree branches. There was a peculiar odor spread throughout the settlement, vaguely unpleasant. He approached the one who had brought the water sac to Vala and sniffed him. These people had their own peculiar smell.

He overheard Enga and Tog speculating about the flimsy dwellings.

I think they might be portable, Tog thought-spoke. *Maybe they move about following their prey.*

That is possible, Enga answered. *Do you remember the Saga of Our Ancestors, the one that tells about the time when they roamed much of the while?*

Jeek had not heard that one for a long time, but now he recalled it. Of course, there was also the Saga of coming to the village from a faraway land. That one was about travel, but Enga referred to another Saga, one that told of the Hamapa when they were not settled in one place and moved to follow the animals they hunted. There were not so many animals at that time as there had been later. All his life, until the recent moon cycles, game had been plentiful, so there had been no reason to move about.

He noticed the strangers conferring with each other. They were clothed in animal skins, as were the Hamapa, but these skins were not mammoth or bear, or even deer. The fur, worn on the outside, looked stiff, like the bristles of a peccary, about as long as bear fur, but not so dark, more the color of mammoth. Jeek wanted to touch one of their garments.

They used only their strange words to communicate, it seemed, and no thought-speak. After many spoken words and some head nodding, one of the males came forward.

He wore a band of woven grasses wrapped around his head. Small river shells hung down in his face so that Jeek wondered if he could see well. His skin was dark, like the others, but his hair was the light color of aspen leaves as they lose their summer hue when they are going into the Cold Season. Several more of these strangers had the same light hair, but most were dark.

The male walked toward them slowly. Jeek looked at his brothers and sisters in puzzlement. Should these people not send a leader to greet them? Why were they sending a male? Maybe the female leader was away from the village, trading or exploring or scouting.

When the male got to them, he scanned their faces. Hama stepped forward. He raised his eyebrows and looked at her mate, Hapa, and at Panan One Eye. Those two stood just behind her, ready to defend the tribe if it was needed. Hapa and Panan both focused their gaze on Hama, ready to take cues from her.

Then Jeek understood. These people were led by a male, not a female. Part of the Mikino Saga, a part that was not always used, told about them having male leadership. But the Mikino were not like the Hamapa at all. These ones seemed more like Hamapa, not Mikino.

Words came from the mouth of the male, but they all sounded like, "Hoody hood hood hoody."

As he spoke, he gestured toward the firepit. Some roasted meat lay on a rock beside it. Jeek thought he might be offering the meat to them, but no one made a move toward it. Finally, the male picked up a piece, lifted it to his open mouth, and pretended to eat it, then handed it to Hama.

She reached up, for the male was very tall, and took it between two fingers. She drew it to her nose and sniffed. Her eyes closed and a look of joy so intense it was almost a look of pain came to her face. She tore a small piece off and tasted it. She chewed and chewed. Then she smiled a huge smile and spoke to him. "Yaya. Ta." She was telling him, *Yes, good, thank you*.

The male pointed to the meat piled on the large, flat rock. The other males and some of the females also pointed to it.

With great caution, the Hamapa stepped forward and took small pieces of the meat. As they began to eat, the others smiled and nodded. Some of the Hamapa began at a slow pace, then ate more and more. They were all so hungry.

At first, Jeek enjoyed the fresh, cooked meat intensely. After the first edge of his hunger was satisfied, he began to think it tasted strange. Almost bitter. It was also tough and stringy. His empty belly rumbled as he ate. But if he chewed it thoroughly, he could eat it. It was fresh, and better than the jerky.

When the pile of meat dwindled, the head male clapped his hands and some females ran to one of the huts and brought out more cooked meat. The Hamapa ate and ate until they could eat no more. They all wondered what this strange meat was, but they knew it had saved their lives.

Hama gestured to the ground, trying to ask if they could sleep there, in the center of their village. No one understood her, so she lay down and raised her eyebrows in question. When the males standing nearby nodded, the rest of the Hamapa tribe lay on the ground also to sleep.

Sister Sun was disappearing as the eyes of Jeek slowly closed. He heard the strange tribe moving about, but nothing seemed alarming. Most of them went into the abodes to sleep, but a few of the males stayed awake, sitting or standing near the Hamapa tribe. Jeek wondered if they were guarding them from something, or if they did not know if they could trust the Hamapa. Neither group knew much about the other one.

Chapter 10

"Jefferson's ground sloth, *Megalonyx jeffersonii*, lived in North America approximately 150,000 to 9,400 years ago… (It) inhabited the lower forty-eight states except for the Rocky Mountain and desert regions… The ox-sized animal (8 to 10 feet long) browsed on leaves and twigs of the woodlands and forests."

—*Ice Age Mammals* by Ian M. Lange, p.82

"Does sloth meat taste good? Not to people living [in] most…parts of the globe. Outside of a handful of indigenous South American tribes, there isn't much of a tradition of eating sloth meat. Researchers who work in Amazonia and have sampled the dish report that it's slimy, chewy and gamey, and most feel that one serving is enough for a lifetime."

—from http://www.slate.com/articles/
health_and_science/explainer/2012/02/
explainer_house_call_what_does_
sloth_meat_taste_like_.html

Enga Dancing Flower felt good when she awoke at first sun, better than she had felt for a long time. There were no pains inside her. Some of the strange dark men sat drowsing nearby. At first, the sight of them startled her, then she remembered encountering the people who said, "Hoody hood hood," and following them to this village where her tribal brothers and sisters all ate their fill of the unfamiliar meat.

The strange tribe members were emerging from their huts, stopping to stretch. The huts were small and there might not be room to stretch inside, Enga thought. She did not think she had to mask her thoughts from these people. She could not penetrate any of theirs, so they could not read hers. They spoke softly to one another, then several of the females walked away from the center of the community. Enga heard high-pitched squeaking noises from beyond the village. There must be animals close by, she thought. Maybe the animals she heard were the ones they had eaten. Curious, she rose from the ground and followed the females.

Three large caves yawned in the hillside behind the village. The entrances were blocked with heavy stones, heaped about as high as the shoulders of these tall people. Soft animal noises came from inside the caves. Enga sniffed for the odor of the animals inside, but could smell nothing. What creature was this that had no odor?

The females saw that Enga had followed them, but paid little attention to her. Cut grasses were mounded not far from the mouths of the caves. The women grabbed armfuls of these and threw them over the stone walls.

The noises from the animals stopped and Enga heard them crunching the dried grasses. She wanted to see what these creatures were, but could not. However, the hillside that held the caves was one of many other surrounding hills. One of these jutted out beside one of the caves. Enga climbed the small incline. As she reached the point where she could see inside, Sister Sun sent a burst of light over the stone wall and into the cavern.

There they were! One was clear to her in the rays of Sister Sun. Enga had never seen such a creature. It was about the size of a muskox, but shaped somewhat like a bear. Several more of them came into the light at the front of the cave where the grasses had fallen. Their bodies were thick and heavy. They rested on their front knuckles when they walked, with long claws pointed backward. When they rose on their hind legs to eat, they were taller than the dark people who held them captive. They grasped the hay with those front claws and stuck the stalks into their mouths. Their snouts were short, their necks and their tongues long.

She caught a few glimpses of smaller ones, probably babies since it was birthing season for many animals. She remained watching them feed, unaware of anything else around her because she was captivated by them. Gradually, she noticed the sound of running water. A small stream made its way down the highest of the series of hills that stretched behind the village. The hills held patches of large trees.

These people were fortunate to have the caves for their animals and also to have water nearby. Enga was stabbed in her chest with a pang of longing for the village they had left behind. It had been perfect. The nearby Sacred Hill had held the Holy Cave where females went to give birth. That cave was where she and Tog Flint Shaper had their First Coupling. That was where the permanent fire was kept. Also young females went to the Holy Hill when they showed the first Red Flow and were becoming adults.

And the Aja Hama had been buried on the Sacred Hill. Most members of the tribe were exposed on a large flat rock far outside the village and given back to Brother Earth and the animals. But Aja Hama had been a special leader, most wise and kind, and had been given a burial. Enga ran her thumb and forefinger over the smooth carving of her that was in her waist pouch.

Then she shook herself out of her longing for something that would never be again and returned to the village with slow steps.

Panan One Eye sat next to one of the tall females. He was letting her stroke his bald head. She wore a wide wrist band made of stone, which slipped up and down on her arm. None of the dark people were bald, as Panan was, so this, Enga was sure, had to be something new and strange to them. Both Panan and the female smiled as she stroked his smooth pate. Were these two going to mate?

The stone band on her arm was beautiful. It looked like it had been shaped and polished. No stone could be that shape by itself. Enga wondered how that had been done.

Enga was interrupted in her thoughts by Hama sending a bright red public message to the tribe. *These people should be called Hooden.*

This seemed like something that Hama would usually tell them in a Pronouncement. She understood why Hama did not want to make one here, in this place, in front of these people. So the thought-speak message conveyed the official name of these people. Hooden. Enga liked the name. It suited them and their speech.

Some of the Hamapa were discussing whether to stay here or to journey on. Hapa and Panan One Eye, the male advisors, called Hama to them. After some private discussion, the three Elders decided they should stay one more dark time, then continue. During that day, most of them rested, still being tired from the long journey with so little food. Once again, as dark time approached, the Hooden shared much food with them.

Enga saw that other females wore the same stone bands she had seen, and many males wore feathers and shells in their hair. This was new to Enga. The Hamapa often braided shells into their hair, but had never used feathers.

At first sun, Hama sent a message that they should go soon.

Enga told Ung Strong Arm and Lakala Rippling Water, who were near, about the stream she had seen, sending them a picture of the water flowing near spruce and hardwood trees on the hills.

Ung gathered some others and they climbed the hill to fill the water gourds in case there was little water where they were going.

The Hooden seemed to understand that the Hamapa were leaving. Their females scurried into their huts and emerged with animal skins. They thrust these at the males.

What is inside? asked Enga of Tog.

He unbound the thong that held the new parcel closed. *It is much more of the meat we have been eating. It is dried, but it smells the same.*

When they all realized they were being given such a precious parting gift, Hama told Tog to give them some of his finely shaped spear heads. But the Hooden did not know what they were and gave them back. Maybe, since they ate the caged creatures, they did not hunt any other animals. Hama then reached into her own pouch and produced some thongs strung with river shells and tiny bird bones. These were extra of the ones she wove into her hair for ceremonial dances. The male Hooden leader accepted this gift with a wide smile, showing his large, white teeth.

Then the Hamapa departed. Enga was sad to leave such a comfortable place. She thought they were probably going to face more hardship.

Chapter 11

"[The Wisconsinian] glaciation radically altered the geography of North America north of the Ohio River. At the height of the Wisconsin Episode glaciation, the ice sheet covered most of Canada, the Upper Midwest, and New England, as well as parts of Idaho, Montana, and Washington."

—from http://en.wikipedia.org/
wiki/Wisconsin_glaciation#
Stages_of_the_Wisconsin_episode

"The Mississippi River…was formed in the most recent Ice Age… This last Ice Age ended approximately 10,000 years ago, which makes the Mississippi about 10,000 years old as we know it."

—from http://www.4rivers.com/
mississippi/info.html

They had not gone far before Jeek and Gunda, who were traveling in the rear, thought-shouted for them to halt.

Enga Dancing Flower looked around to see one of the Hooden females running after them. It was the Hooden female who had befriended Panan One Eye. When he saw her, Panan ran out to greet her. He took both her hands and they stood like that for a moment. Then, holding hands, he led her to the tribe. The step of Panan looked like that of a much younger man. His limp was gone. He had not had a mate, had not even mated with any female, since the old Hama, Aja Hama, had died. Vala Golden Hair might have wanted to, but Enga was almost certain they had not coupled.

Hapa frowned greatly when he saw them. He sent a thinly veiled message to Panan. *We may not have enough food for us. If this one travels with us, how can we know that we will have food for her?*

We are saved because of her people, Panan countered. *I am old and do not require much meat. I can share my portion with her.*

61

Hapa sent some private thoughts to Hama, who returned them, both of them frowning. It turned out that Hama was disagreeing with her mate. She sent a public thought-speak message, *The Hooden female stays with the Hamapa. She looks strong and we can always use another strong female.*

Enga had doubts about that. She kept the thought to herself that the Hooden females did not hunt. She was not sure this female would be useful. But Hama had made up her mind. The Hooden female journeyed with them.

The land they traveled through held many small streams, some rolling hills, and the spruce and hardwood forests Enga had seen from the hilltop. The next few days were pleasant. They had plenty of meat and could drink their fill of water whenever they got thirsty. Sister Sun was shedding more and more heat on them, but they could cool off in the shady groves. Even Sooka, the fussy infant of Vala, seemed more content, although Vala herself shot looks of poison at Panan as he traveled with the Hooden female.

One day, more of the beasts that had been in the caves were spotted. They moved slowly and always moved away from the people. Fee Long Thrower or Ung Strong Arm, or others, could easily have speared them, but they were all growing weary of the taste of that meat. If only they could find a large herd of mammoth, or even some deer, bear, or bison. Liquid formed in the mouth of Enga when she thought about the taste of mammoth meat, cooked over a searing fire so that it was crispy on the outside, soft and moist and flavorful on the inside. With plenty of water and with the gentleness of Brother Earth, they might be able to settle near this place—if they could find a supply of meat.

Hama sent the young males to the tops of the hills sometimes, to see what they could detect in the distance. What they could see was always more of the same terrain, and never a herd of mammoth or anything else.

They speared rabbits on occasion and even brought down birds and squirrels. These were small, though, and did not feed many.

Eventually, herds of pronghorns, bison, and musk ox were seen. Stag moose were seen once. But the process to build a trap, drive them into it, and corner these for a slaughter, was more complicated than they could do and would take more time than they had while traveling. Three times lone mastodons were spotted in the great distance. The tribe was tempted to go after them, but Hama and Hapa both argued that they would be gone long before the hunters could reach them. They had always depended on mammoth and that was the animal they must find.

They still had the dried meat from the Hooden. The only person who enjoyed eating it was the Hooden female, but they all ate it.

At one dark time, as everyone was preparing to sleep at the edge of a spruce forest, Panan One Eye asked Hama if he could give a name to the Hooden female who traveled with them. Hama discussed this with her mate. Hama and Hapa were quick to reach a decision.

Hama gathered the Hamapa in a sitting circle and thought-spoke to the tribe while pointing to the strange one sitting next to Panan, *That one does not need a name. She is not one of us.*

Enga saw the puzzled look on the face of the Hooden female. She could have no knowledge of what they were discussing, but could see that she was being pointed at and that the Hamapa thoughts concerned her.

Panan countered, *We have always taken in those who come to us. We took in Bodd Blow Striker and Fall Cape Maker. We also took in Enga Dancing Flower and Ung Strong Arm.*

Hapa was quick to answer. *Enga and Ung were infants. Bodd and Fall are people like us. This one is not like us. She is tall and dark and narrow. She does not follow our ways. Can she understand or send thought-speak? She probably will not ever breed or bear a child for us. What work can she do?*

Panan jumped to his feet. *She is a person. She must have a name. Hama is the one who said she could travel with us and—*

Hama stood, too, and raised her chin at him. *Travel, yes. But I have decided she will not be useful, not knowing our ways. She will not live with us when we reach our new place. She will have to find her own kind then. Dakadaga will not name her.*

Enga watched Vala Golden Hair during this public argument. At some of the dark times, Panan set up his sleeping place between Vala and the Hooden. At other times, he was very close to Vala and the Hooden had to find her own place. But some dark times were spent with the Hooden female and Vala was left alone with Sooka. At those times, Vala was not far from where Enga and Tog slept. Enga thought that Panan and the Hooden may have been coupling.

As the days wore on and the trek continued through the same kind of land, tempers again grew shorter and shorter. One day, at a mid-sun rest under some large shrubs, Enga heard soft weeping. She pushed through the brush and followed the sound. The sobbing sounds stopped as she approached. Someone was in distress and Enga wanted to see if she could help, but did not want to startle whoever it was. Making deliberate noise as she parted and snapped branches, she kept going.

She pushed one last thick, leafy branch aside and saw the Hooden squatting on the ground, huddled against one of the thicker tree trunks. The Hooden turned up her dark, tear-streaked face and sent a plea to Enga. The female could not send thoughts, but her look conveyed a plea that was clear. Her eyes spoke of sorrow.

Tears sprang to the eyes of Enga and she knelt to put her arms around the female. *How lonely she must be with no one to communicate to.* She smelled different than a Hamapa, but not too much different. Her skin felt the same as the skin of anyone, even though it was not the same color. Since she was now dressed in Hamapa mammoth skins, given to her by Ung Strong Arm, she did not appear very much different either. Her skin was darker, she was taller, and her very short, dark hair curled up against her head, but those were small things.

The female trembled under the touch of Enga. Was she afraid of Enga?

"Tiki hoo," Enga murmured. The words had arisen unbidden from her mind. They meant, "large one." The woman grew still and drew her head back to look Enga in the eyes. Enga said the words again out loud. "Tiki hoo."

The female smiled, showing a row of even white teeth, large, like the rest of her. She pointed to her chest and repeated the words Enga had said, but making them sound like one word, "Tikihoo." She tapped her chest again and again and said, "Tikihoo."

Finally, Enga understood. The female thought her name was Tikihoo. Maybe it was. Dakadaga had to pick names for the Hamapa, but not for this one. Hama had said that would not happen.

Enga tapped her own chest and spoke, "Enga." She left off the rest of her name, not wanting to make this too complicated.

The other woman nodded and tentatively repeated, "Enga."

Enga took the hand of the female as they stood. Together they brushed through the branches and returned to the tribe.

Enga, still holding the hand of the female, raised both their arms into the air and sent out a public thought-speak message: *Ba Tikihoo*. The heavy stone band that the Hooden always wore slipped up her arm. For emphasis, Enga spoke the name aloud, "Tikihoo," still holding up the arm of the Hooden female.

Panan One Eye rushed to them. He hugged Enga, then hugged the female. *Tikihoo*, he greeted her, then remembered that she did not receive thought-speak, so he, too, spoke the name aloud, "Tikihoo."

Enga saw many smiling, nodding faces. But not all smiled and nodded.

Chapter 12

"The Sawatch Range of the Rocky Mountains was formed around 70 million years ago during the Laramide Orogeny (mountain building). A trough of late Paleozoic sedimentary rocks running through central Colorado was uplifted as a massive dome to create this mountainous range. Drainage off this range, then, created streams; these began flowing eastward, forming valleys. The Arkansas Valley is the northernmost of these valleys and conclusive geologic evidence establishes that this valley was formed no earlier than 29 million years ago."

—from Origins and Geology of the Arkansas River,
http://salida.com/salida-best-of/
best-of-arkansas-river.html

Both Hama and Hapa stood back, frowning. Enga Dancing Flower observed the Hooden female beside her, regarding each member of the Hamapa tribe. Tikihoo ended by staring in the direction of the two high leaders, Hama and Hapa, and a look of fear crossed her face. Her smile returned when some of the Hamapa swarmed around her and gave her gentle pats on the arm and the shoulder.

Panan One Eye came to stand beside her and she seemed content with that, so Enga slipped away and confronted Hama.

Are you angry that I have named the Hooden female?

Hama did not answer. She pursed her lips, raised her eyes to Mother Sky, and looked like she was thinking about whether she was angry or not.

Enga was frightened that she had done something wrong. She tried to explain. *It was not what I meant to do. She wept and wept and I comforted her. When I spoke those words, I only wished to communicate. She is lonely here. She has no one to speak with. No one can understand her and she cannot understand us.*

The expression of Hama changed. Her dark eyes grew kind and her mouth relaxed. *Ah. So you were comforting her and called her "tall one, large one" and she thinks you gave her a name.*

It made her so happy.

You are a gentle person, Enga Dancing Flower. It will do no harm to call her Tikihoo. Dakadaga will understand. Hama touched the mind of Enga with softness and warmth.

Her mate, Hapa, heard the conversation, but did not quit frowning. He thought-spoke with harshness to both of them. *Dakadaga will not understand. And that female will become part of our tribe. We will run out of food in less time. This is the fault of Panan One Eye. He did not make her understand that she could not come with us when we left her tribe. No good will come of this.*

Hama ignored his thoughts and approached Tikihoo to give her a soft pat, as the others were doing.

For the next few suns, Panan slept near Tikihoo and even mated with her openly. Vala Golden Hair wept often. Her green eyes, so pretty at most times, were ringed with red. She ignored Sooka, her child, and the others had to take care of the helpless infant. The males were the ones who did most of the dragging of the heavy loads, so the females usually watched after Sooka. Some of the males were taken with the child and liked to tend her also.

One very warm day the task fell to Enga. The girl would not stay content for more than a few moments. Enga watched Whim dart and dash on his chubby legs and wished Sooka would learn to walk. What if she never did? Whim saw a bird and jumped to try to catch it. He was younger than Sooka, but had been walking for several moons.

The skin of Sooka was light, even more light than that of Vala. The beaming of Sister Sun made her glow with the color of sunset. Blisters had formed on her face and arms at the beginning of the trek. Now the females covered her arms with skin wrappings, which she tried to pull off, but her face still suffered.

The day Enga had charge of Sooka, Gunda, the oldest birth-daughter of Hama, spotted a small peccary and managed to spear it. At dark time, the children gathered sticks from the ground of a copse nearby. With the permission of Hama, Akkal took a bit of his fire and lit the branches to roast the meat of the peccary. There was only enough for a few bites for each person. Enga closed her eyes to chew and sensed the joy of the whole tribe at the taste of fresh, familiar meat.

When they were finished eating, Zhoo of Still Waters, the Healer, collected much of the fat from the animal and put it in her pouch. Next she rubbed some on the sore face of Sooka, who smiled and cooed when the fat relieved her pain. After that, Zhoo smeared some on Sooka's face every night. In the morning, she renewed it and also patted some dirt on the fat. That kept most of the fiery fierceness of Sister Sun from burning the baby.

For some time after Enga had given the name Tikihoo to the Hooden, Hapa went from one brother and sister to another, complaining about Tikihoo being with them. He would not use the name Enga had given her, but called her the Hooden. He laid much blame on Panan. He even blamed Panan and "the Hooden" for the fact that they were not yet in a place where they could settle.

Enga was alarmed that Hapa did not try to conceal any of this. She could tell that feelings were growing against Panan in some of the brothers and sisters. That was, she thought, caused by what Hapa kept repeating. She heard mutterings about Mootak Big Heart being made the official Storyteller, the Hava, and taking the job away from Panan. But Panan continued to give the Saga most of the time when they stopped walking at early dark.

In the mind of Enga, there was a worse thing than Hapa spreading the ill feelings. And that was the role of Hama. She did nothing to counter the division in the tribe. Some were deciding to mutter against Panan, as Hapa did, and others defended him. Hama could have stopped the arguments and dissension, but she did nothing. Enga thought that Hama must be as weary as they all were.

But this was not proper. Panan had been an Elder of the tribe for a long, long time. He was the mate of Aja Hama when she was alive. He was the seed giver for Lakala Rippling Water, for Fee Long Thrower, and for Tog Flint Shaper. These three were all important members of the Hamapa. After the Aja Hama had left Panan and had mated with another, Panan remained one of her trusted advisors until her death. He deserved respect.

It was most important that the tribe be in agreement. If they did not stay together, they were not likely to survive. Their numbers would be too small and they would not have enough people to do all of the tasks of the tribe.

So why, Enga wondered, did Hama not stop Hapa from spreading bad thoughts? Was she too tired? Was her spirit worn out?

* * *

One day the two birth-brothers, Teek Bearclaw and young Jeek, were sent to the top of a nearby hill to scout the land. Jeek was proud to be chosen for the mission. They scaled the hill in a short time and looked in every direction.

Jeek was agitated about what they saw, jumping up and down when they spied it, although it was not good news. They ran down the hill to tell the tribe. Teek said Jeek could announce it.

A very large river is ahead, Jeek thought-spoke.

How large? Hama asked. *Is it wide? Deep?*

Teek answered. *It looks wide. I cannot tell if it is deep. But it does not look like there is a way around it. It flows across our path and blocks us for as far as we could see in both directions.*

Both Teek and Jeek sent out pictures of what they had seen.

How wide do you think it is? asked Hapa. *I cannot tell from your pictures since you were far away from it. Can we build something to take us over this river?*

I think we cannot, but I do not know, Teek thought-spoke. *It is wider than either Fee Long Thrower or Ung Strong Arm can throw a spear. It may be that we can wade through it.*

Let us hope that is true. Hama nodded at them for a job well done, even though the news was not good. *How far away is this water?*

Jeek and Teek looked at each other and conferred in private before Teek answered. *Maybe one more day of walking. Maybe two.*

As they trudged onward, more weary than ever, toward a destination that might be a big problem, Jeek could tell there was much unhappiness about other matters. Some were muttering against Panan, others against Hapa. Those two were rivals now for the favorable thinking of the tribe members. Hama called a halt for the day as Sister Sun was disappearing before them. Brother Moon was bright and had been showing his face for many hand lengths of Sister Sun through Mother Sky. Now he winked down at them, along with the many eyes of Dakadaga, shedding light so they could see well.

They were not yet at the bank of the river. It would be one more sun before they reached it. There was much fear about what they would do when they got there.

After they gathered in the usual circle, Panan once again was asked to give the Saga. He chose to give a short well-known one about Beaver.

I will tell of the Saga of the Giant Beaver of ancient times. In the times that are the most dim in the memories of Storytellers, there lived a Giant Beaver, an Enormous Beaver, more great than the ones who live now.

Jeek sat near Mootak Big Heart. Mootak poked Jeek with his elbow as the Saga started. He sent Jeek a private message. *This is not the right Saga for this time. A Saga of river crossings would be better. Or maybe one of meeting obstacles as a tribe and working together to figure out our problems.*

Jeek could see that Mootak might be right. But what good would those thoughts do?

Mootak Big Heart, we must be careful not to divide the tribe any more than it already is. We must not speak against the leaders.

But I should be a leader. Not Panan One Eye. He is too old. With his one eye, he cannot see what should be done. I would do the job much better. I know all the Sagas. When Panan One Eye calls me to learn them, I do not go.

Had Mootak made fun of the one eye of Panan? That was not good. Jeek closed his mind to Mootak and listened to the continuing Saga of the Giant Beaver and of Creation.

He was given a task by Dakadaga, the Spirit of Mother Sky. Her child, Brother Earth, was covered with swirling waters and there was no dry land. Dakadaga and Beaver dove to the bottom of the waters and brought up piles of mud. They shaped the mud into hills and valleys.

Jeek began to think that Mootak might be wrong. This Saga was about creating rivers. It was suitable for this time when a river was on the mind of everyone.

Then Dakadaga built mountains and caves while Beaver made paths for the water so it could run in rivers and streams. Beaver sent water over the mountains to make waterfalls, and dug deep holes to make lakes.

Panan stopped the Saga there and did not go on to tell of Beaver invading villages and devouring people. That was a good part to omit. The Hamapa did not need to be reminded of things that would eat them at this time. The ending, Jeek remembered, was that Dakadaga commanded that beavers only eat fish.

I told you, Mootak thought-spoke to Jeek. *There are no beavers in that river. It flows freely and has no dams.*

Jeek told Mootak that he did not want to hear any more. It took him a long time to fall asleep that night.

Chapter 13

Everyone knew that they would reach the riverbank at the end of the next day of trekking. To Jeek, it seemed that they walked more and more slowly as Sister Sun sank before them. No one wanted to reach the wide water.

At last, they were standing on the banks of the river. It was not far below them since the banks were short and not steep. Sharp rocks stuck out of the water here and there, creating ripples and pleasant musical tones.

Hama summoned Bahg Swiftfeet to her side. She had a private conversation with him. He nodded. Bahg gave a long look to his mate, Fee Long Thrower, who held their baby boy. Then he walked down the small slope and put one foot into the quickly flowing stream. Jeek hoped that Bahg would not be swept away by a deceptive strong flow beneath the surface.

It is not too cold, Bahg sent back for everyone.

He took another step, and another, until the water reached just under his arms. He was not yet halfway across.

Come back, Hama summoned. *It is too deep to wade across. We will have to cross it some other way.*

Discouraged, they sat and ate the hard, tough, dried Hooden meat. Soon, Hama told them to go to sleep without a Saga. Jeek wondered if that was the idea of Hama or of Panan. There was much grumbling about not having a Saga. Jeek thought it was a mistake not to have it. The Hamapa needed encouragement. They needed their spirits lifted. Going to sleep with no Saga, no singing, no dancing, was not the way to do this. But he was not an Elder and would try not to think against them.

Everyone began laying out a place to sleep in the open, beside the noisy flowing water, since no trees lined the banks. Jeek had not slept well the night before, and he could not sleep now either. He crept off and strolled away from the tribe. He found a deer path through the nearby woods and followed it for a short length. He was thinking of turning around to go back when he was surprised to find Gunda ahead of him.

He stopped and thought-spoke softly, *Gunda, what are you doing out here?*

And Jeek, you? Why are you out here?

I could not sleep. There are so many troubles.

Gunda nodded in agreement. Her birth-mother was the Hama and her seed giver the Hapa, so Jeek did not expect her to say anything against them, about how they were causing some of the troubles.

But she surprised him. *If only Hapa would quit talking about how awful Panan One Eye is, and about how we should not let Tikihoo travel with us.* She stared at him with those deep, leaf-colored eyes. The light of Brother Moon caused them to glint like water. *Or maybe Hama should make a Pronouncement. Or maybe there should be a meeting about this matter.*

I agree. Something should be done. There is nothing you or I can do. The Elders must guide us and lead us.

Gunda agreed with that also. *Come, comfort me.* She opened her arms and Jeek stepped closer. They embraced for a long time. Water flowed from the eyes of Gunda.

They touched their lips together. Jeek thought that he might melt into Brother Earth. In all the blackness of the moment, this was a spot of brilliant light for him.

They walked slowly back to the encampment, holding hands.

At first sun, Jeek was reluctant to get up. Gunda, curled up nearby, slept on while the others stood and packed up their things, as they had done every day on the trek. However, there was nowhere to go this day.

Some of the female spear throwers ventured into the trees to see if they could catch fresh meat. Two of the males went with them, in case they found something large and speared it. The males would be needed to carry it back if such a wonderful thing happened.

The other Hamapa sat, got up and walked around, and sat again, aimlessly.

Jeek tried very hard to think of what they could do. He could clearly see the other side of the water. It was not far. But there was no way to build anything to cross the river. It was much too wide for that. If they could see the other shore, Jeek thought, they should be able to reach it. But how? If only they could find a beaver dam and walk across it.

Jeek was startled out of his thoughts by an unusual noise. He looked up to see two males grappling with each other, grunting and making sounds like animals. Hapa wrestled with Panan! Now Hama must do something!

Hapa threw his fist into the face of Panan, then Panan grabbed the arm of Hapa and bit down. They both yowled louder and each kicked at the other.

Hama ran to them and put her hands on their arms, but Jeek did not think she was very quick to do it.

Thoughts flew through the tribe.

This is terrible.

Hamapa do not do this.

Now Hama will call for a meeting.

Hapa is so wrong to talk against Panan One Eye.

Panan One Eye should step down and let Mootak Big Heart take his role.

Do not speak against Panan One Eye. He is our Elder.

Hapa is our Elder. We should listen to him.

For every opinion, there was a Hamapa throwing out an opposing one.

After Hama separated the two males, though, she did not call for a meeting. She did not even scold them. She turned her back to everyone and shuffled away from the river, scuffing and dragging her feet. She stood by herself for a long time. The rest of the tribe turned away to give her some privacy. Here, on this trek, they had no wipitis where they could go to be alone.

When Jeek saw her shoulders shaking, he knew she was weeping, even though she did not let her thoughts escape. A Hama must always be good at keeping private thoughts.

At dark time, again, there was no gathering. No Saga, no song. Jeek felt he was not the only one who lay awake, troubled.

At first sun, Enga Dancing Flower sent a message out to everyone. *We need help. We must get guidance from Dakadaga. Help me ask for blessing and a passageway around or across this water.*

She drew a carved figure from her pouch. Jeek recognized it, as did everyone else. Stitcher had carved it. The wood, smooth and polished, looked like Enga had rubbed it much. She set it on the ground and began to dance in a circle around it.

Ung Strong Arm and Fee Long Thrower joined Enga. Lakala Rippling Water began a soft tune. The song became stronger, pleading for help from Dakadaga, The Most High Spirit. More joined in the dancing. Then Lakala sang praise to Wawala, Spirit of the Waters. Sannum Straight Hair had no drum to beat, but he pounded his feet on the earth to create a rhythm.

Hama approached. She sat outside the circle of dancers and watched.

Everyone looked to Panan One Eye. He should play his flute, Jeek thought. But Panan sat beside Tikihoo, watching Vala Golden Hair dance with Bodd Blow Striker. The Hooden put her fingers on the face of Panan, touching the darkening mark that had been made by the fist of Hapa.

No one comforted Hapa. The Red had flowed from his arm after Panan bit it, but soon stopped. Now there was a welt. Zhoo of Still

Waters had packed some pieces of grass onto it, covered that with the fat from the peccary, and dabbed a bit of her precious honey on the top. That had worn off during dark time. The wound did not look serious, Jeek thought. Sometimes, when an animal bit a Hamapa, the wound became bad and the Hamapa could even lose his life from it.

More and more of the tribe joined the dancing. Soon everyone but Panan and Tikihoo were whirling around the wooden figure. Vala Golden Hair shot looks of poison at Panan and Tikihoo. Her thoughts leaked a bit and Jeek picked up a wave of animosity. Panan turned his back on Vala.

It was strange to dance while Sister Sun shone. Jeek did not remember ever doing this before. He held the soft hand of Gunda as they whirled, helping the notes of the Singer to reach the Spirits so they would send them the help they were desperate for.

Chapter 14

Enga Dancing Flower, the best dancer in the Hamapa tribe, danced for her life—and also for the life of her tribe. They must find a way across the wide water. There was not enough game or even plants here to support them. She whirled faster and faster, rejoicing when the others joined in. She dipped and bowed, arching her back then flinging her fire red hair. Surely Dakadaga would notice them dancing at this odd time, at high sun.

In addition to Dakadaga, she danced to other Spirits that might help them, Wawala, the Spirit of the Waters; Puka, the Spirit of Strife; even Ka, the Spirit of Brother Earth. Those pleadings were sent so everyone could hear them, but she also sent out cloaked pleas to Aja Hama, even though she was not a true Spirit. She cloaked these thoughts in case the other Spirits might get jealous that Enga was beseeching Aja Hama, a mere Hamapa.

She kept dancing until she was out of breath and a pain stabbed her midsection. Enga stood to one side, out of the path of the other dancers for a moment. She closed her eyes and swayed to the sounds of the music. The notes of Lakala Rippling Water were pure and true. Sannum Straight Hair did his best to provide a beat. The only thing missing was the flute of Panan One Eye. Her breathing slowed and the pain lessened slightly. The odor of sweat came from the writhing bodies. The smell of her brothers and sisters was comforting.

Enga, rested now after her brief pause, rejoined the circle of dancers making their way around the Aja Hama figure, taking the place of the usual campfire. Could the Spirits see them without a fire lighting the dark time of Mother Sky?

Panan sat, impassive, being comforted by Tikihoo, the Hooden named by Enga. Had Enga angered the Spirits by usurping that task and bestowing a name? No, they should not be angry. She did not intend to bestow the name. The Hooden misunderstood. She named herself. Enga had not done that. She had not angered the Spirits, she was sure. Hama had agreed with that. Who knew what Spirits watched over the Hooden? If any were to be angry, it would be those, not the ones Enga knew.

If any Spirits were irritated with Enga, or with the Hamapa, then she just had to dance harder. Still, she addressed Aja Hama with her most private shades of thought.

They whirled and dipped in their ragged mammoth garments, many of them with filthy, dusty arms and legs and faces, their hair straggly and loose. None of them had dipped into any water for many, many suns. Would this dancing hold any appeal? Would it help them? They thought that they must do it, on the chance that they might catch the attention of a Spirit who could get them across the water.

Sister Sun beat down hotter and hotter. Some fell. Some had to stagger to the riverbank and drink water. Enga was determined not to stop. She lurched into Tog Flint Shaper and grabbed him around the waist to remain upright. She smiled up at her mate. Then noticed that Vala Golden Hair, who had been with Bodd Blow Striker, now had a hand on his arm. Vala smiled at Enga, but it was not a warm smile. A chill came over Enga, even in her overheated state, standing in the full sun. Enga, with her arms still around Tog, pulled and turned him away from Vala, and he returned the embrace of Enga. A wave of hot anger flowed from Vala as she drew her pretty face into an ugly sneer that Enga caught over the shoulder of Tog.

Vala stumbled and fell into Tog. Tog had to let go of Enga and support Vala so she would not fall. Enga danced off, away from them. Vala had intended to fall against Tog. Could he not see that? Every time she looked, Vala was close to Tog. Enga danced faster, spun and spun and spun until the ground tilted.

* * *

How could Enga Dancing Flower dance so long? Jeek did not understand how this would help the tribe. They needed to get across the river, not to dance until they fell down and could not get up.

Jeek had to sit and rest long before Enga did. Most of the tribe took twice as many breaks as Enga did. It was growing dark and many wanted to quit, but Enga urged them on.

At last Hama stepped in front of Enga. *It is time to rest. We must all rest now.* She thought-spoke to Enga so that everyone could hear, but softly, in the colors of the sky and of pure, shallow water.

After that, they quit dancing, one by one, but Enga was the last to stop.

Jeek slept very well that night, except when some vivid visions came to him. The visions were of the flowing water, and of Jeek sitting on the bank thinking. There was a vision of him leading the tribe across the river. The river of his sleep was narrow and shallow.

When he awoke at first sun, he ran to the river. It was still very wide and flowing swiftly.

As soon as everyone had chewed a piece of Hooden jerky, Enga again started dancing. This time she held the Aja Hama figure high, so everyone could see, and she led most of the tribe in another circular, unending dance. Tog Flint Shaper pulled her out of the dance and thought-spoke with her, but she shook her head and resumed, leaping and twisting even more than the day before.

Tog sent a harsh message to her that everyone could pick up. *You must rest. You must drink and eat. You will lose our baby.*

Enga ignored her mate and kept on.

By dark time, the Hamapa were exhausted. Lakala had stopped singing long ago, after her voice grew scratchy and hoarse. Sannum occasionally drummed out a weak beat with two sticks he had picked up that day. The dancing of Enga had turned into a dirt-kicking shuffle. Most of them stood in one place and swayed, heads hanging down and eyes closed.

Now there was grumbling because Panan One Eye had done no dancing. Most thought he should dance also, not stroll around with

Tikihoo, resting, going off into the woods, and giving no help with the infant Sooka or with Whim, the small child of Fee Long Thrower and Bahg Swiftfeet.

Some, though, did not think the dancing would do any good. No response from the Spirits had been received. This was the most dancing they had ever done at one time. If the Spirits had not answered by now, there was no use continuing.

Sister Sun continued to burn them with her hot eye and they could almost see the grasses withering around them. Jeek thought the water mocked their dancing with its gurgling and splashing on the rocks in the middle. Mother Sky did not send her breath to stir the leaves or to dry the damp hair of the dancers. If anything, Jeek thought the Spirits might have turned against the Hamapa.

When Enga started dancing again the next day, Jeek had to leave so that his angry thoughts would not betray him. *This is not right. This is not the way to cross the water.* Those thoughts whirled in his head like the dancers whirled in the dirt. He kept them cloaked in the darkest shade he knew, that of Mother Sky when Brother Moon was not there and her cloud garments hid her eyes. Out here, on this trek, there was not even the central fire that had always burned in the Paved Place. He used thoughts of that darkness to help guard his thoughts.

He walked into the woods and stopped, breathing in the coolness of the shade and the lush smell of the growth, trying to calm his mind.

Where are you going? Gunda had come up behind him.

I do not know exactly. I want to follow the water. You could get your spear. We could look for game.

The others have looked. No one has found any for several suns.

Everyone was so exhausted that Jeek did not know how much effort they had put forth. *We can walk all day while they dance. We can find food.*

The eyes of Gunda glowed and she smiled like Sister Sun. She ran back to retrieve her spear and they trotted into the woods, keeping within the sound of the water so they would be able to find their way back.

Jeek felt that his steps were lighter than they had been lately. He stole shy glances at Gunda, smiling when she returned them.

After they had traveled along the river for a bit, Gunda pointed at the dark cloud garments far ahead of them. *If we go too far, we will get wet.*

That is very far away. Those clouds are not moving toward us. Jeek scuffed his foot against the hard, dry ground. *It has not rained here for moons, I think.*

By the time Sister Sun was directly overhead, they realized they had not brought anything to eat. They had stopped twice to dip their faces into the river and drink, so they were not thirsty. But Jeek knew that Gunda could hear the sounds his hunger was making inside him.

Gunda halted and put up her hand. *Do those look like berry bushes?*

They were! Jeek and Gunda ate their fill, foraging into the forest, then sat and leaned against two tree trunks. Jeek felt drowsy and his vision from his dreams returned, the vision of leading the tribe across the water.

Should we go back to our tribe now? asked Gunda.

He shook off the lethargy, but the vision persisted. *I want to walk a bit more. I want to look at the water. Then we can tell everyone about the berries.*

Gunda followed him through the spruce and poplars toward the bubbling of the river.

Walk with me a little ways more, Jeek thought-spoke. He wanted to be alone with Gunda longer.

The shore of the river here was crowded by the forest. They stepped carefully along the banks so they would not fall in. Jeek heard a difference in the water ahead. After a short distance they parted the trees and came to an open space beside the stream. The water flow was quite narrow here. Jeek looked back the way they had come. The waterway had been narrowing as they had moved upriver. He could see the banks spreading out and widening behind them.

We could walk across here if it is not too deep, Gunda thought-spoke in a burst of joy and golden color.

Jeek stepped into the water and took a few steps. It swirled gently around his legs. He made it to the middle before it reached his waist. His joy was so great that he sent out brilliant, radiant pictures of himself in the water. He waded on to the other side.

We must tell the tribe! Gunda exclaimed. *I will send pictures to them also.*

Chapter 15

"They could certainly communicate, as can all social animals, and they no doubt spoke, albeit simply and probably slowly."

—In Search of the Neanderthals
by Christopher Stringer and Clive Gamble, p. 217

"Many anthropologists came to believe that Neandertals could have spoken any modern human language, whatever their accent may have been."

—The Neandertals: Of Skeletons,
Scientists, and Scandal
by Erik Trinkaus and Pat Shipman, p. 391

Enga Dancing Flower saw that everyone was stopping. Just as she was about to exhort them to put more effort into the dance, she received the thought-pictures that Jeek and Gunda were sending to everyone.

Hama herself let out a screech. Her grin was almost as wide as her face. *Bahg Swiftfeet and Teek Bearclaw, do you have strength to run? To see what the young ones have seen?*

It seemed everyone was renewed by the thought that they would be able to get to the other side of the river, at last.

The two males nodded. They checked with Jeek and Gunda for more information on their location and took off for the woods that bordered the water.

Enga collapsed onto the ground. Her sobs were quiet, but her birth-sister, Ung Strong Arm, always tuned in to her emotions, came and squatted beside her. Ung draped her muscular arm around the shoulders of her birth-sister. Enga wept harder. The mate of Ung, Lakala Rippling Water, ran over to them and helped soothe Enga.

I am going to be fine. I am joyous. I am relieved that my dancing worked.

It *was* her dancing, she knew. Dakadaga, or maybe Wawala, the Spirit of the Waters, had shown Jeek and Gunda where they could cross.

Her tribal brothers and sisters were mostly squatting or lying on the ground, breathing hard and recovering from the dancing. They regarded her with curiosity. Several of them sent her cautious messages of gratefulness for her dance. A few sent thoughts of scorn that she would take credit for what Jeek and Gunda had done.

In spite of that, Enga knew she had saved the tribe.

Sister Sun journeyed almost one hand length through her Mother Sky before Bahg and Teek sent back thought-speak messages that they had found the two youngsters. The four of them stood at the edge of a narrow stream in the picture they sent.

Bahg sent the thought, *I have seen young Jeek wade to the other side. We can all cross here.*

Hama summoned them. *Come back now. We will rest through the coming dark time and will cross at first sun when we are fresh.*

Hapa had been gazing at his feet. He looked up. *Let us go to the place where they are. We can camp there. It is not far. From the scene that Jeek and the others sent, we can see there is a clearing that lies beside the stream. It looks large enough for us to stay there for one dark time.*

Hama considered this for a moment. *What you say is good. We will then be fresh as we start across the water. We must be alert and be careful. The water can conceal many things.*

It was agreed, then, that they would make their way through the dense woods and rest before attempting the crossing. Hama made it clear that she would decide whether or not they should cross there, but what else could they do? Warm, grateful feelings flowed to Jeek and Gunda.

* * *

Soon Jeek could hear people coming through the thick growth. He basked in the glow of the pride he felt from Gunda.

The birth-brother of Jeek used to be called Teek Pathfinder because of his skill in tracking and finding game to eat. His name was changed to Teek Bearclaw after he survived an attack by a bear that left deep scars on his back. It was understood that someday Teek would become the Healer, after their birth-mother passed the role to him. Before this trek had started, Teek had studied much with her. He would take that up again when it ended. Jeek wondered, with the most private colors he could manage, if he, Jeek, could become Jeek Pathfinder at his Passage Ceremony. No one had that name now, although Teek was still skilled at it. Jeek had three summers to go, but the tribe would remember how he led them over the water until then, would they not? He was lost in thought, contemplating the ceremony and his new name.

Gunda poked him with her elbow. *They are almost here. I will run out and guide them the last part of the way.*

I will go with you! He must show them the way. He would not be named Pathfinder if it was not clear that he had found the path.

When the tribe followed Jeek and Gunda and saw that there was room to camp, and that the stream looked safe and shallow, relief flowed from every sister and brother. The older men clapped Jeek and Gunda on their backs.

Gunda sent out a public thought. *This was found because of Jeek. He is the one who insisted we come here.*

Jeek had feelings of love for Gunda so intense that they burned his chest. They flowed like water from his eyes. He wiped his eyes with the back of his hand. Then he grabbed Gunda and hugged her tight.

He thought, for a small moment, that he and Gunda had forgotten to tell the tribe about the berries. They would not want to go back to that place now, though. It was not near.

Enga Dancing Flower approached, smiling at them.

Jeek, what made you go here? How did you know this crossing would be in this place?

He hesitated. Would she understand? It was not something that usually happened. He always trusted Enga. So he told her. *I dreamed about this. When I was sleeping, I saw a crossing like this one and I saw myself leading the Hamapa across the water. I could see it as clear as I am seeing it now, at this moment. It looked very much like this place.*

Enga nodded, accepting this vision.

* * *

Enga Dancing Flower was overjoyed about the vision of Jeek. She knew that a Spirit had come to him in his sleep and given that sight to him. That had happened because of her dancing. It was because the tribe did so many Asking Dances and because Lakala Rippling Water kept singing for so long. The Spirits might have let them find this place sooner if Panan One Eye had played the flute.

She felt a cold wave and turned. It came from Panan. She had let a bit of her thought spill out and he had received it. He frowned at Enga and turned back to Tikihoo.

Tikihoo was pointing to the water and saying the same thing over and over. "Ayoo. Ayoo. Ayoo."

Enga wondered if that sound meant *water*. It was possible that, since she did not seem to have any thought-speak, she had to use clumsy spoken words for everything. It was reasonable that she would have a spoken word for water.

Panan repeated the sounds. "Ayoo, ayoo, ayoo." He pointed to the water and she nodded with vigor.

Enga thought the word might mean "fear" because Tikihoo looked frightened when she said it. Everyone had noticed the storm cloud garments at the edge of Mother Sky. They did not threaten the Hamapa in this place, but Tikihoo glanced at them as she kept repeating her one word.

Hapa sent Panan an angry thought. *Do not rejoice. You did nothing to help find this place. We should leave you on this side with the Hooden.*

Enga waited for Hama to correct him. Her back was turned and she was speaking to some of the females. She had to have received the thought of Hapa. It was strong and full of venom. Enga had not been this worried about the unity of her tribe since before the last Cold Season— when the Hama was killed.

Chapter 16

At dark time, Enga Dancing Flower lay on her pallet with a heaviness deep inside. Pains shot through her body, but the pain of her spirit was worse.

Ung Strong Arm left the side of Lakala Rippling Water and squatted beside her birth-sister to stroke her hair. *The color of sunset and leaves at the end of the summer*, thought-murmured Ung. Ung wiped the tears from the face of Enga with her wide fingers. At that, Enga had to give her a weak smile.

Tog Flint Shaper had been beside Enga when they first lay down, but had gone to help Vala Golden Hair with the unruly little Sooka. Bodd Blow Striker had been with Vala and Sooka, but had gotten up and was pacing a short distance away. Eventually Tog noticed that Enga was in distress and came to her. Ung left as he walked over to his mate.

He thought-spoke privately with Enga. *Are you in pain?*

The pain is not very bad. My spirit is in pain, though. I am worried about our Elders.

Tog put his broad hand flat on her stomach, where their seed grew. *I can feel pains here. Your muscles are cramping. I will get Zhoo of Still Waters to give you something.*

Enga grabbed his hand. *No, do not do that. There will be time enough to tend me after we are across the water.*

Are you going to lose our baby? Enga could see the dark shade of fear in his thought-speak. It made her happy that he was looking forward to loving the baby as much as she was. He was adept at dealing with Sooka. He would make a good parent.

No, no. I will not lose the baby. Enga hid her doubt from him.

Tog curled up next to his mate and they took comfort in each other through the dark time, though neither slept much. At some time during the night, Mother Sky started sending bright spears down, lighting up the night sky, and giving out the rumblings she always sent with the spears. Enga hoped the rain storm was not coming toward them. Not until after they crossed the water.

When Sister Sun began her trip across her Mother Sky, she sent a beam onto the eyelids of Enga. Enga turned her head away from the light before sitting up and looking around. Hama and Zhoo of Still Waters were stirring. Everyone else slept.

At last, a bright red message from Hama went out, shot with the white-hot of a lightning bolt from Mother Sky. *Arise, Hamapa! We must cross the water. Mother Sky gathers her dark garments and will weep on us soon.*

Enga looked up. Hama was right. Sister Sun still hovered close to her mate, Brother Earth, and shone clearly now. But she would not continue to for long. The most dark garments of Mother Sky, laden with water and growing more and more large, would soon crowd out the light. Mother Sky blew a cold breath from the direction of the cloud garments. She was telling them to hurry.

They all knew that if Mother Sky wept too much or for too long, this river could gather much water and rise out of its banks, even in this narrow place. They had seen that happen to the stream where they used to dwell, although their village was positioned so that it would not flood. This place was next to the water. It would flood if the water left its banks. That would not do. Not this day.

With much haste, Tog helped Enga stuff her things into her carrying pack, then he helped the others gather up the large dragging pack. The most strong males decided to carry it together over the stream, balancing it on their heads. Tog, together with Bahg Swiftfeet and the two Gata males, hoisted the pack and waded into the water.

Enga was dismayed to see that the water was higher than it had been the day before. Mother Sky must have shed tears upstream. The water had only reached the waist of young Jeek when he showed them the crossing. Now it swirled around the waists of the grown males and was growing more deep as they watched. All of the younger ones would have to be carried.

Tog returned to help Enga across, since she told him how weak she felt. He carried her pack and held her arm. She could feel smooth rocks and sharp rocks, some large and some small, on the bottom of the stream bed. Two times she slipped on a smooth one and Tog held her upright. It was a slow process, crossing the stream. She had to be careful where she placed her feet. The current seemed to be growing more strong also, making her and Tog lean against it to remain upright.

Hama and Hapa had three offspring, Gunda, and two younger girls. Those were of eight and ten summers. Hapa was able to carry each one across, one at a time. Cabat the Fat was then helped by Tog. Cabat was old and not steady on his feet. Sannum Straight Hair carried the two small offspring of him and Ongu Small One. Fall Cape Maker, the tall Gata, carried Ongu since the water would have covered part of her face. The river was now up to the chests of the males. It grew ever more deep.

The tears of Mother Sky, at first soft and gentle, beat down more and more hard and fast. The wind blew cold. Those who had crossed and were wet shivered on the other shore. They would not have the heat of Sister Sun to warm them or to dry their clothing and did not know how long they would be so cold.

One by one, the others continued to cross, some helping others, some carrying the loads of others, until a roaring, rushing sound was heard. They all knew what that meant. The ones who had crossed gathered everything and ran away from the water.

Enga hoped those still on the other side would be able to outrun the flash flood also. She did not have time to see who had crossed and who had not.

When they had all gone enough distance to reach a high enough spot, they stopped.

Enga looked behind her and saw trees and brush that had grown alongside the stream being torn out and swept along, with chunks of mud being washed from the banks. The torrent looked angry. Were the Spirits still not pleased with the Hamapa? What more could they do? Enga did not think she could dance another step.

Who is not here? Hama asked.

Zhoo of Still Waters thought-spoke, *My birth-son, Teek Bearclaw, is not here.* Jeek puckered his face and looked about to cry. He was frightened for his birth-brother.

Ongu Small One and Sannum Straight Hair both reported that their son, Mootak Big Heart, was on the other side. He had been helping with the very old and very young ones. They clutched the hands of their two younger sons as they conveyed their messages.

After accounting for everyone else, it was decided that Panan One Eye and Tikihoo had been left stranded, as well as a few who had returned to help them. These were Hapa, Mootak Big Heart, Teek Bearclaw, and Fall Cape Maker.

Hama shot a message to the stranded ones. *Have you all made it to safety?* She named those who were missing.

Hapa answered and told them that, indeed, those people were the ones with him. They were all safe for now. They had gone to a dry rise, past the woods, which was now filled with flowing swift water.

The water will be too high for you to move until next sun, Hama thought-spoke. *Do you have any meat with you?*

Tikihoo carries a small bundle with some dried meat.

We will wait here until it is the right time for the rest of you to cross. Hama motioned them to make camp where they stood. They were unsheltered, but it would be good to remain close enough so that they could keep watch on the river.

The dark time stretched out more long and more dark than most of them that Enga could remember. Since Panan was not there, Vala, with Sooka, nested next to Bodd Blow Striker. Enga huddled with Tog and also with Ung and Lakala for warmth. Others clung together, wet and quaking with cold, waiting for first sun. Enga hoped the water would go down by then, but she could hear it rushing as the rain continued to fall on them and into the waterway. What had been a narrow stream, now was a rushing river.

Chapter 17

When the water at last receded enough for the others to cross, two suns had passed. Their clothing had dried during the first sun.

Enga Dancing Flower worried about the crossing of the others. The water was again low enough to wade through, but it would be hard to see the way. The water was not clean. But also, Mother Sky and Sister Sun worked together to warm the air so quickly that thick mist rose from the river. Enga could not see the other side. The mist spread a dense fog out from the water until they were all enclosed by it. Their dry clothing was getting wet once more.

Hama had communicated with Hapa, though, and they had decided the others were going to cross over, with some help.

The banks were both littered with branches, tree roots, and piles of brush, up to the flood line where the water had reached. Most of the Hamapa who had already crossed stayed where they were on the rise, but a few made their way through the debris to the edge of the water, disappearing into the whiteness. Hama called Sannum Straight Hair, Tog Flint Shaper, and Bahg Swiftfeet to come with her in case they needed help, and then picked her way through the fog and the debris. As they left, Vala Golden Hair grabbed Sooka and trotted after them. Enga thought she must be concerned about Panan One Eye. Another thought occurred to Enga. Vala might want to greet Panan and claim him, since he had now been with Tikihoo for two suns. How would Bodd Blow Striker feel about this?

Hama sent back a steady stream of pictures, although Enga could see very little, mostly fog. The three Hamapa males stayed on the near shore. Fall Cape Maker sent a message that he would help Tikihoo first. As he crossed, he let everyone know that the river was more deep than it had been, but was still passable. It was not as swift as he had thought it would be.

It seemed like a long time until Enga could see, through the mind of Hama, Fall and Tikihoo emerging from the fog, wading the last short distance that was visible, and climbing the bank. They stood shivering from the cold water in the damp air, waiting for the others to cross.

Since Teek Bearclaw and Mootak Big Heart were both younger and might be frightened, Hapa decided to help them across. He would bring Teek first. He and Hama thought it best for them to cross one or two at a time, as they had done on the very first crossing. The path through the water where they could get footing among the rocks was not wide.

Hapa waded into the water and was lost to view as the whiteness closed in on him. Another long time passed until Hapa and Teek appeared. These were long-time members of the tribe, not like Fall and Tikihoo, so joy sprang from those around Enga, and from Enga herself, that they were safe.

Now only Panan One Eye and Mootak Big Heart remained to be rescued. Hapa said he would go back to help Mootak next. There was a long delay, more long than the other times, when Hapa did not send back anything. Hama shot questions across the water. *Is Mootak Big Heart all right? Are you all right, Hapa? Tell us what is happening.*

At last Hapa thought-spoke to all of them. *Something bad has happened. I will bring Mootak Big Heart across and you can hear it from him.*

Soon the sloshing was heard of Mootak and Hapa wading back. Hapa helped support Mootak, who was having a hard time walking. When they got up the littered slope, Hapa let go and Mootak collapsed amid the branches and mud piles left by the flood. His face was pale. Dirty tears streaked his cheeks. He swiped at them with a muddy hand. Mootak was small, like his birth-mother, Ongu Small One, but had the straight black hair of his seed giver, Sannum Straight Hair. That hair, wet and dripping, hung over his sorrow-laden face as he bowed his head.

Sannum knelt beside him and put an arm around the shoulders of his son. *Can you tell us what happened?*

Mootak did not answer.

Panan One Eye is not there, Hapa thought-spoke. *Mootak Big Heart was there alone. He cannot tell me what happened to Panan One Eye.*

Let him rest a bit and give him some more time. Hama knelt on the other side of the young man and stroked his hair. *Something terrible must have happened.*

Thought-pictures of animals, or even Mikino, attacking Panan sprang into the mind of Enga. Or maybe, she thought, he got swept into the water and carried away.

Mootak looked up at last, and his eyes opened wide. He bent his legs and wrapped his arms around his knees, tight, and rocked back and forth. *It was a Spirit. A white Spirit. An evil Spirit.* He paused.

No one moved. The Hamapa all knew that evil Spirits existed. Those battled with the kind, ruling Spirits that the Hamapa acknowledged and praised and danced for. But they did not ever talk about them. Speaking of evil Spirits might draw them closer. They all held their breath, mouths closed, so that the evil Spirit would not enter into them.

Are you certain? Hama asked.

Mootak nodded. *It was white all over. It came out of the mist and...and...* He started shuddering with such violence that he had to stop sending his thoughts. He squeezed his eyes closed, but they flew open again and he made a low whimper.

What did...it do? Hapa thought-spoke. *Is Panan One Eye harmed?*

He is dead! It struck his head with a rock. Over and over. With a large rock. Then it pushed him into the water and vanished.

Enga felt a wave of horror go through her tribe mates. Had Mootak seen a true thing? Or had the swirls in the fog looked like something else? If Panan was truly dead, she did not think a Spirit had killed Panan. A person would look white from a distance in this mist.

Soon they all returned to the rest of the tribe. All but Hapa. He went back across the water to find Panan. By time the wet people had all been wrapped in what extra garments and skins that could be found, Hapa was on the other side. He sent a message for someone to help bring back the body of Panan.

He did not send a picture. Instead, he used thought-speak only. *I did not have a hard time finding Panan One Eye. He is floating near the shore, caught in the roots of a tree that washed away in the flood. His life has left him, as Mootak Big Heart said. His head has been smashed and a rock lies near him, higher on the shore. It is covered with his Red. I do not think a Spirit did this. They do not lift rocks and attack with them.*

Enga agreed with that. Who had Mootak seen? All white he said. Could it be Stitcher, the very white tall one who had left the tribe? Had he returned? Why would he want to hit Panan? Some of the Hamapa were pale also.

Tog and Bahg returned to help Hapa carry the body. Sannum and Ongu Small One comforted Mootak as he sat and rocked, front to back, his eyes still wide, the shock and horror rolling off him in heavy laden sheets.

Chapter 18

"[At] La Brea tar pits…about 70 percent of the fauna are carnivorous mammals and birds of prey… They include the gigantic Merriam's teratorn (*Teratornis merriami*). This extinct, meat-eating relative of the stork weighed 30 pounds and had a 14-foot wingspan."

—*Ice Age Mammals* by Ian M. Lange, pp. 27–78

After the body of Panan One Eye was brought to the place where the rest of the Hamapa were gathered, Hama decided on the first action. *We will dispose of his body and sing for him.*

Should we delay for this? Hapa asked. *It is important that we keep journeying after stopping so long on the other side of the river, and for the flood.*

Hama answered, *He was an Elder and deserves the respect of a burial. He should be buried to protect his body from scavengers. We should cover ourselves with ashes and mourn Panan properly.*

We also should *dress him in camel skin and sprinkle him with flower petals*, Cabat the Thick thought-spoke. *We should* dig *a deep hole and spend many suns chanting and moaning.*

Hapa considered this, then shook his head. All knew they would not be able to do most of this. It would take time to bury him and they had already stayed in this place, crossing the water and waiting for the flood waters to go down, for too long, as Hapa had pointed out.

All were gathered around the body, but Enga Dancing Flower noticed that Tikihoo stood apart. She did not look at the body, but gazed into the distance, back toward the river.

After a private conference between Hama and Hapa, Hama thought-spoke to all. *Panan One Eye is an Elder. However, we cannot bury him properly. He will be left to return to Brother Earth and the animals that live here, as we do for those who are not Elders.*

Enga thought she detected satisfaction from Hapa that Panan would not be treated according to his rank in the tribe.

Hama asked if anyone had animal fat to spare. Zhoo of Still Waters thought she could spare a bit. There was no wipiti to take Panan into for privacy, so his clothing was stripped where he lay. Zhoo dabbed some of the precious bear fat she had brought from their village onto his skin. She even used a bit of the peccary fat she carried to protect the tender skin of Sooka from the rays of Mother Sun.

Several scouted for a suitable place to lay him. They did not find a large flat rock. That would have been a good place. Bodd Blow Striker said he saw, in the distance, odd projections coming up from the ground, but they looked very far away. Enga squinted toward the far edge of Brother Earth. There were the sharp gray forms.

If those are rocks, they are not flat, she thought-spoke to Bodd.

He agreed and trotted off to join the others who were still looking for a place to expose Panan.

At last, they decided to leave him upon the ground. There was no other place. The body was carried a short distance and laid onto the ground with reverence. Everyone came to the place but Tikihoo. She remained behind and had still not looked at the body of Panan.

Lakala chanted a short Song of Asking to the animals of this place, asking them to take the Hamapa brother for their use.

When Sister Sun returned, she would dry up what was left of Panan after the night creatures had nourished themselves. Already, a large bird was wheeling above them, casting its shadow over the group. They gave a collective shudder and moved away.

They decided to continue and walk as far away from this place as fast as they could. They did not want to hear the sounds of beasts feeding on Panan in the night. Perhaps that bird overhead was not going to wait for dark time. It circled more and more low.

As they started out, Sister Sun returned, pushing aside the dark, heavy clouds, and warming those who had been in the water most recently. The strange, distant, blue-gray forms continued to intrigue them, but the tribe seemed to draw no closer to them, even though they walked until long after Sister Sun had gone to mate with Brother Earth for dark time.

If only Enga could talk to Tikihoo about why she avoided the body. That was puzzling Enga.

During that dark time, everyone slept well, Enga thought. She slept soundly herself. The pains where the baby-seed rested stopped bothering her at last.

When she awoke, Hama was summoning them to awake and eat some of their jerky so they could begin walking again. Some rose and started chewing the tough, odd-tasting stuff, but some did not. Enga was startled to intercept the dark mood of Hapa and the hostile look he gave to Hama. The air between them bristled with dissension.

She was even more startled to realize that Ongu Small One and Sannum Straight Hair seemed to be sending defiant private answers to Hama. This stream of thought was kept private, but these four were not happy with each other, that was clear. The oldest child of Ongu and Sannum, Mootak Big Heart, huddled on the ground where he had slept between his parents. His two younger brothers wrapped their arms around him, but Mootak shook with such violence, it was difficult for them to do this.

Enga realized that Mootak was still suffering from what he thought he saw, a Spirit killing Panan.

* * *

Jeek answered the summons of Hama to rise and eat, and started to chew his jerky while he packed away the skin he had slept upon. When he looked around, he saw, just as Enga had, that not everyone answered the summons.

He observed Mootak Big Heart. Mootak did have a tender heart and was a good member of the tribe most of the time. But the mind of Jeek was filled with the recent thoughts of Mootak, the thoughts that he wanted to replace Panan before it was time. Mootak had even jeered at the one eye of Panan. Panan had lost his eye on a hunt long ago, when a spear went astray. That was not a thing to belittle. Was Mootak afraid that the Spirits would punish him for having bad thoughts about Panan, now that he had died?

Then another idea came to Jeek. Did Mootak hit Panan with the rock? Did he make up the story of the Spirit in the mist? If Jeek had done that, he would be terrified of being found out and would also be lying on the ground shivering.

Jeek stopped what he was doing and squatted to think about his idea, his eyes closed and his face in his hands. Mootak had been alone with Panan on the other side of the water. They had been alone long enough for him to do this thing. It had taken Hapa some time to help Teek Bearclaw across. Both Jeek and their birth-mother, Zhoo of Still Waters, had been in close communication as Teek crossed in the deepened water, worried about him and making sure he was safe.

Ongu let her thoughts to Hama go out to everyone to be heard. *Look at Mootak Big Heart. He can not travel. He is in deep distress. We must stay here and let him rest and recover before we move on.*

Jeek knew that Mootak would feel weak from the herbs his mother, the Healer, had given him to help calm him. Was that his problem? If there were some way to carry Mootak, they could leave, but each person had a bundle and most were weakened by the trek. Jeek thought no one would be able to carry Mootak. He was small, but not small enough to be a light burden.

Hama pointed to Sister Sun. *Sister Sun is moving into position for the Cold Season. We can not stay in one place any longer. We must go forward. We must find the mammoth. If we do not, we can not live through that time. We will run out of the meat from the Hooden.*

Hapa squinted up at Sister Sun. His long hair hung loose down his back and glistened in the light from Sister Sun. He frowned at Hama and let his difference with his mate be known. *It is not proper for us to continue on the journey and to lie all together at dark time when one of us killed Panan One Eye.*

A fresh ripple of fear disturbed the minds of all. Contradictory and confusing thoughts flew back and forth at once.

An evil Spirit killed Panan One Eye.

We have no more killers in this tribe.

No Hamapa killed Panan One Eye. It was a Spirit.

It was the newcomers.

Mootak Big Heart saw the Spirit.

The Tikihoo woman killed him.

Enough! Hama commanded them to quiet their thoughts. *We must go now. We will have a council tonight to discuss this.*

Cabat stood next to Hapa and folded his arms in front of him, a deep scowl on his wrinkled face. *How can we go when we have a killer with us? We cannot go.*

Cabat was acting as an Elder. Did he think he should be the third leader, since Panan was gone and Mootak was not functioning?

Jeek was scared. It was never good when the Elders argued with each other. The tribe depended on their guidance and wisdom. Without agreement, there could be no guidance. He watched the three stare at each other.

Hama strong, but not tall. Not many Hamapa had done what she had, killed lions by herself. But Hapa, her mate, towered over her. His name had been Donik Tree Trunk and he was nearly the size of a tree. Cabat the Thick had a gravity of his own due to his heft.

Hama, Hapa, and Cabat walked away from the tribe to discuss their difference. Jeek hoped they could come together soon.

However, they stayed away for nearly two hand lengths of Sister Sun through Mother Sky. It was near the middle of the day. If they did not start soon, there would be no point in setting out, only to travel a short distance before stopping for the dark.

Cabat returned alone, not letting any of his thoughts be seen. Jeek thought that Hama might have dismissed him from their meeting. It had been many moons since Cabat had been an Elder. Maybe Hama and Hapa did not want to treat him as one.

Sister Sun beat down on them, all sitting in the open and far from any trees. Jeek was hot, but he saw that Mootak still trembled as if he were freezing.

Gunda came to sit beside Jeek. He was sure that she was much more upset than he was, since the leaders were her parents. He took her small, soft hand in his and rubbed her back with his other hand. He was rewarded with a grateful smile beneath her tear-filled green eyes.

A shout of thought-speak went out. *They are back!*

Gunda and Jeek both looked up. Hama and Hapa walked back to the tribe, but slowly. The head of Hama hung down and her jaw was clamped tight. That was not a good sign.

Without looking at her mate again, Hama addressed her tribe. *We will not walk today. It is necessary to hold a council now, in the middle of sun time. If we do not do this, we will split the tribe.*

That filled Jeek with a lump of cold, dark dread, and he knew everyone else felt it, too.

No! We must never split the tribe! Enga Dancing Flower was on her feet and her eyes blazed with feeling. Tog Flint Shaper tugged at her garment to quiet her. She swatted his hand away. *We will die if we do not stay together.*

There was much agreement for what Enga stated. Hama nodded also. *Then our minds must meet in the same place.* She glanced at Hapa and he squatted next to Cabat while she stayed standing. Enga sat as everyone else, and Hama did also.

Hama continued. *Panan One Eye is dead. His head was smashed with a rock. He was put into the water and the rock was left on shore with his Red upon it. There are two things that could have happened. A Spirit killed Panan One Eye. Or a person killed him. That is the first thing all must agree on.*

Heads nodded. Jeek let out his breath. At least the tribe was trying to come together on something. But how could they agree on one of those options?

Mootak Big Heart will tell us again what he saw, Hama thought-spoke. *Then Hapa will tell us what his idea is.*

Jeek looked at Mootak, now sitting up and paying attention to everything that was going on. Was he still sick? Or had he been sick at all?

Chapter 19

"Several...species of pronghorns lived during late Pleistocene time and died near or at the end of the epoch, about 10,000 years ago... Extinct species of pronghorn that lived during the Ice Age include members of the genus *Tetrameryx*, meaning 'four horns' in Greek. These animals had two horns with two prongs on each stem."

—*Ice Age Mammals* by Ian M. Lange, p. 143

Sister Sun moved closer and closer to Brother Earth. Her light grew less and less strong. Soon they would kiss. She had been keeping closer to him lately, even in the middle of the day, getting ready for the cold season. Hama was correct that they must move on. They were not in a place they could stay for Cold Season.

Enga Dancing Flower exchanged a few private thoughts with Tog Flint Shaper about what Mootak Big Heart said he saw, and about what Hapa thought.

What is your idea? he asked her.

I will wait until I hear what they both have to say.

You are wise, Enga Dancing Flower. I will do likewise.

Mootak Big Heart was helped to his feet by Sannum Straight Hair. Sannum continued to support his son, encouraging him to speak, to tell what he had seen.

It was hard to see. Mootak tilted his head back and looked straight up, into the abode of Dakadaga, where a tiny sliver of Brother Moon glowed dimly. Enga wondered if he was seeking help. *This is what I saw—*

What you think you saw, interrupted Hapa.

Mootak Big Heart will have his say, Hama thought-spoke with a stern dark blue tinge to her thoughts. *Then you will have your turn, Most High Male.*

Hapa turned his head away from Hama and it looked like he bit back all his thoughts, compressing his lips together.

Mootak continued. *The mist was thick. Panan One Eye had gone to the edge of the water to get a drink. He was not near me. I could not see him well. A white Spirit rose up from the water, as white as cloud garments worn by Mother Sky in the middle of the most bright day. The Spirit picked up a heavy stone. She crept up behind him and bashed Panan One Eye in the head. Then she bashed him again. He fell to the ground. The Spirit rolled him into the water. I did not dare to confront the Spirit. I could feel evil coming from her. I had to close my eyes and did not see where she went.*

Mootak collapsed and Sannum guided him into a sitting position. He fell over into the lap of Ongu Small One.

Enga knew the Healer had been looking after Mootak and she wondered why he was not yet over his terror. She wanted to talk to him after the meeting and ask him some questions.

Hama stood and thought-spoke to all. *A Spirit does not kill one person from behind with a rock and then put him into the water. That would have to be a most great Spirit, an evil one, one of Rocks and one of Water and of Death, all together. There is no Spirit like this.*

Hapa stood up, looming over them. *Mootak Big Heart, I know you saw a Spirit lift a large rock and kill our Elder with it. There are some who believe a Spirit cannot do such a thing.* He did not look at Hama as he spoke. *I hope the Spirits are not listening to us now. Spirits are mighty. A Spirit can cause the side of a mountain to slide and that can bury someone, or cause a big wind to blow and destroy dwellings. Why could a Spirit not lift one rock and kill one Elder?*

Enga was surprised that Hapa had changed his mind. Maybe Cabat the Thick had influenced him. If only all three of them could agree, it did not matter to Enga what they agreed on. The tribe must come to a consensus and move on. That was the most important thing.

Hapa looked around at the tribe to see if they agreed with him. Some tilted their heads in thought, considering, others nodded, some frowned. Enga held herself still, pondering the words of Hama, of Hapa, and of Mootak. Some questions occurred to her. They were more questions for Mootak that she would try to ask of him later, in private.

Cabat stood up with a grunt. *Does any Hamapa know every Spirit? We know many of them, but have they all been revealed to us? No other person was there, only Panan One Eye and Mootak Big Heart. If this great, evil Spirit did not kill our brother, then it must be that Mootak Big Heart did that. But did he? Can anyone say he did that? Look at him!* Cabat thrust his pudgy finger at Mootak, now curled up in the lap of his birth-mother, shivering as hard as ever. *Can anyone say that this young man killed our Elder? That is the choice, if the Spirit did not. Would he be this frightened if he had not seen a great evil Spirit, a Spirit not only of Rocks and Water, but of Death? A great White Spirit, a Spirit of Mist.*

Enga saw Mootak quit shivering and pay attention to what Cabat said. Many, many heads nodded. In the end, Cabat the Thick, an Elder who no longer had a position of power, a heavy-set Hamapa who loved to eat more than anything else, convinced most of them that such a Great White Spirit existed. A Spirit so evil none had ever seen Her before.

There were a few who did not think the reasoning of Cabat was true. There was no flow of agreement.

Enga was one who did not agree. Her birth-sister, Ung Strong Arm was another. Their eyes met and, with slightly lifted eyebrows, they sent their doubts to each other. However, no one dissented to everyone and it was agreed that a person did not kill Panan One Eye. Hapa did not agree, but he did not give any more of this thoughts.

We will ponder these things during dark time, Hama thought-spoke. *At first sun we will come to an agreement.*

Enga did not approach Mootak after that. Her mind was too troubled. There was no agreement now. Would there be later?

At first sun, Hama searched every mind. She kept to herself what she was finding out. Enga tried to search some herself, but most Hamapa held their minds closed to her, to anyone but Hama.

When Hama had gathered the opinions of everyone, she stood and raised her arms upward to give a Pronouncement. Her face was tense and her body stiff.

"Hoody!" she began, as always. "Yaya, Hama vav."

Listen! Yes, the Most High Female speaks.

"Hamamapapa no yaya. Mana too. Hamamapapa poos, vava yaya."

The Hamapa do not agree. We stay here. The Hamapa will leave when all agree.

All throughout the day, the mood of the tribe was low. Small groups gathered together and some tried to change the minds of others.

Cabat and Sannum both spoke with Enga. It was difficult for her to differ with them, but she could not agree with either view. She did not think a strange, unknown Spirit killed Panan, but she did not know whether Mootak did it or not.

At high sun Enga felt her pains returning. She walked out from the dismal tribe. Her pains seemed better when she moved, even though it was hot, walking. At least her mind felt better, being away from the secretive, soft thought-speak murmurs, making the air shimmer with their discordant vibrations. She walked with her head down, lost in her own gloomy thoughts.

A sudden movement straight ahead made her look up. A strange deer bounded across her path and disappeared over a slight rise. The animal had four horns on its head, two horns pointing forward and two pointing up.

Excited, she turned back toward the tribe to transmit a picture to Ung Strong Arm of the strange deer with many horns. *Maybe you and Fee Long Thrower and some others can go after this creature. There may be more of them nearby. Those animals usually run in herds.*

Ung transmitted the thought that she would call others, grab her spear, and run to the place where Enga was.

Enga spied someone trotting toward her. But that person was not Ung. It was Hapa.

I have been looking for you, he thought-spoke directly to her. *You know that the tribe must move on. We must reach agreement. There are many who think that there was an evil Spirit. I do not think so. Neither do you. We are the only ones.*

Why was he saying all this to her? She knew there was one other, Ung, and maybe Tog, but Hapa did not know this.

I have a proposal, for the good of the tribe.

The good of the tribe was always the most important consideration. She listened intently to Hapa as she caught sight of Ung and Fee running toward her carrying their spears.

We must all agree, he continued. *If we agree that there was such an evil Spirit, we can move on.*

And the person who killed Panan One Eye? Enga asked. *This might be Mootak Big Heart, but it might not be him.*

Enga had had the unwanted thought that Hapa could have killed Panan. He said he found Panan dead, but he could have killed him, if what Mootak saw was not true.

Hapa answered. *I do not know. As we travel, we can find out who it was. Will you help me? You are the one who helped find the killer in our midst once before. Can you do it again?*

She was confused by Hapa taking one view, then another. These were confusing times, but was Hapa speaking his true thought? Whether he was or not, the plan of Hapa was the best thing she could think of. She agreed to do that. She would seek out the thoughts of all her brothers and sisters and see if she could find the hidden, dark, wicked corner that sat in the mind of the killer.

I, Hapa, will give you any help you need.

Enga nodded. Ung and Fee had reached them.

Where is this strange beast you saw? Ung asked.

Enga pointed over the rise and the two hunters trotted off to try to find it. It had been large and fast, so Enga was not sure they would get near enough to throw their spears.

Chapter 20

"There is no better herb [than mother-wort] to drive melancholy vapors from the heart; to strengthen it, and make a merry, cheerful, blithe soul, than this herb is.

"Mugwort soaked in water, is very useful to strengthen trembling hands…"

—*Indian Doctor: Nature's method of curing and preventing disease according to the Indians* compiled and published by Nancy Locke Doane, pp. 36 and 49

"Mugwort is a plant that grows in Asia, North America, and Northern Europe. The plant parts that grow above the ground and the root are used to make medicine… It is also used as a liver tonic; to promote circulation; and as a sedative."

—from http://www.webmd.com/vitamins-supplements/ingredientmono-123-mugwort.aspx?activeingredientid=123&activeingredientname=mugwort

Ung Strong Arm and Fee Long Thrower returned to the others long after Enga Dancing Flower and Hapa got back. They had found a herd of the beasts, but had only managed to catch up with a small one. The animals ran fast and were gone before they could lift a spear.

No one wanted to start a fire here for this one small kill, so the bit of meat that was shared was eaten raw.

To Enga, it tasted wonderful, even uncooked. It wasn't the dried Hooden jerky. Anything tasted better than that. She had a thought, that they had had enough raw meat recently that she might get used to it. Then she changed her mind. She would always prefer cooked meat.

Before the two hunters got back, Enga and Hapa had announced their agreement that an evil Spirit was the killer. After that, all agreed and it was decided they would leave at first sun. Enga was glad others had not changed their minds. At last, they would be able to get on the way to the new land.

Zhoo of Still Waters had given to Mootak Big Heart more of the healing and slowing herb she carried in her medicine satchel. He sat calm and still, no longer trembling. Enga knew his parents were relieved about that.

Hama decided to have a council meeting as darkness fell. They gathered in a circle around the remains of the small antelope. It was mostly a pile of bones now, but it had given them pleasure. Lakala Rippling Water started with a Song of Thanks to the animal. Enga was surprised when the Gata male, Fall Cape Maker, picked up the flute of Panan and began to play along with her melody. Sannum beat two sticks together for rhythm and Enga could almost imagine that she was back in the village. Some day, all of this would happen in a new village. Sannum would have a large hollow log to beat and maybe Fall would be the new flute player. The notes he blew from the flute sounded tuneful and sweet.

Mootak swayed with the music. He should be playing the flute, taking over for Panan, but Enga did not think his lessons on the instrument were complete. Would he give the Saga tonight? When Hama beckoned him, he rose, slowly. He was going to give the Saga. Enga was glad of that.

He began by announcing that he would tell the Saga of the High Places. This, they all knew, told of impossibly high passages their ancestors crossed many, many summers ago. More summers than could be counted.

Mootak started strongly.

The brothers and sisters saw the High Places in their path. They could not get around them. They must go across, over the tops of the high peaks. It was with great trial that they...that they climbed and climbed and climbed. It took many...many...many moons...

Mootak shook his head.

The Saga is ended.

He sat, with shame on his face.

Zhoo of Still Waters, who had given him the healing and slowing herb, soothed Mootak. *Do not be ashamed, Mootak Big Heart. The medicine I gave you will not let you continue. You did your best.*

Still, Mootak was disheartened that he was not able to complete the Saga. He radiated his feeling of disgrace.

If Hama knew he had been given the herbs, Enga wondered why she called on him for a Saga. It would have been more wise to omit it for this council. Everyone was suffering on this trek.

At first sun, when Hama awoke and told everyone to get ready to leave, it was evident that Mootak could not yet travel. This time it was because the calming medicine had had a great effect on him. Zhoo looked worried. She touched the back of her hand on his forehead, then laid her cheek against it. She stared into his eyes for a long moment.

No, he cannot travel today, she thought-spoke. *Maybe at the next sun.*

Enga was disappointed. She and Hapa had announced their false conclusion just so the tribe could proceed. She would use this one more motionless day to seek out the thoughts of her tribe. Maybe the person who hit Panan with a rock would let a stray thought slip out when idle and off guard. That was a terrible, heavy deed to hold inside and not to share. It must be weighing someone down.

She noticed Ung and Fee conferring together. Soon, they left for the rolling hills where the antelopes had been. They were gone most of the day.

Enga went from one chattering cluster to another. They were all conversing about different things. Some wondered what they would find ahead. Several speculated on what the distant gray shapes were.

Maybe Mootak Big Heart is wise beyond his years, Ongu Small One, his birth-mother, thought-spoke. *Do you think those are the High Places of the Saga?*

They are small. They are not high, Jeek answered.

But they might be very, very far away, his birth-brother, Teek countered.

That same subject was much discussed by others also.

Vala Golden Hair and Bodd Blow Striker played with Sooka. Bodd was gentle with the child. He would hide his face behind his hands, then take them away with a sudden sound, which startled Sooka and made her laugh. That was a game all Hamapa babies liked. Enga stopped to play with the baby also. Sooka was delightful when she was happy. She rolled a pine cone to the child, landing it between her chubby outstretched legs. Sooka then picked it up and tried to roll it back. They both laughed at the game. Enga left her with a smile on her face. But she had not picked up any dark thoughts from Vala or Bodd.

Her mate, Tog, stood conversing with the other Gata, Fall Cape Maker. Tog was interested in how Fall made his special capes, by lacing them with thongs in an intricate way, crossing the leather strips over each other to be more secure. The only things on their minds were capes and laces. She would never think Tog had killed Panan, but Fall was new to the tribe and no one knew him well yet.

She wandered to others, stayed awhile at some, passed by others, always tuned in to their thoughts as acutely as she could be. Nowhere, in any of the minds, could she find a dark, hidden spot that would tell her who was the killer.

Discouraged, she squatted by herself, with her own thoughts. They went in the direction of the seed of Tog that she carried. She started to smile at these thoughts.

Then, without warning, her pains began again. Fear gripped her. She was becoming afraid her seed would come out too soon and would not live. She looked around for the Healer, but she was tending Mootak. She must approach her later and see if there was anything she should be doing to keep the seed inside her.

When Sister Sun was sinking low, Ung and Fee came trudging back. In the distance, Enga could see that Ung bore a bulky weight across her shoulders. Could it be? It was! It was a full-grown antelope. Enga started drooling at the thought.

Even Hama ran to greet them and to help carry the animal. *How did you catch up with this? It is a fast animal, you told us.*

Fee nodded. *They are fast. But not clever.*

Fee and Ung told of scooping dirt for a long time to form a depression deep enough to hold the adult animal. This took them most of the day. Then Fee drove the herd toward it and one fell in. As it struggled to get up, Ung, standing ready nearby, threw her spear.

After they ate, there was dancing and music at the gathering. It was almost like old times, although there was still no fire.

* * *

Jeek was jittery, which was unusual for him. This was like the time when someone had killed their leader. He had wondered then how well he knew the people he lived with every day. He found himself wondering the same thing now. How could a Hamapa be that deceptive? How could anyone kill Panan One Eye? All respected him, even when they differed with what he thought. As an Elder, he could state his opinions, no matter what they were.

Jeek studied Mootak Big Heart in the faint light from Brother Moon, who was not nearly full this night. Mootak, now the Hava, the only Storyteller, no longer trembled nor lay curled up in a ball. But his manner now was not too much better. He sat not far away with his back against a tree, his legs straight out in front of him, and his eyes held a film that looked like one of the thin, wispy garments of Mother Sky. The Healer checked on him often. Jeek knew she was worried, too. She let Jeek know that she was afraid she might have given him too much of the calming herb.

Jeek stole close to Mootak, not wanting to startle him, and brought him a drink from his gourd. He stayed and sat with him, hoping to comfort him. Mootak was in no condition to control anything, even his thoughts. The thoughts were weak and wispy, like the clouds in his eyes, but Jeek could decipher them.

This is my punishment. I am being punished.

What are you being punished for, Mootak Big Heart? What have you done? Jeek did not want to hear that Mootak had killed Panan, but he had to know.

Creatures of the dark time moved in the woods behind them, rustling the fallen leaves beneath the trees that were dropping leaves and beginning to prepare for Cold Season. The woods smelled like rodents and other small animals.

I am being punished for thinking such awful thoughts about Panan One Eye. He was an Elder. I should not have wished him ill. I even made fun of his one eye.

You are correct, Mootak Big Heart. Those were wrong things. But if you are being punished for that, surely your punishment will end soon. Is there anything else you should be punished for?

Mootak looked at Jeek with horror. Even in the dim light Jeek could see that the film was gone from his wide-open eyes. *You also? You think I killed an Elder?* Mootak jumped up. He started pacing back and forth, his energy suddenly returning.

Jeek assured him that he did not think so. Mootak had professed his innocence with so much vigor, but was it too much vigor? He had asked, *You also?* Did others think that? Would Mootak again become agitated and need more of the calming medicine? If he did, they would not be able to leave at new sun. Jeek spent some time soothing Mootak and telling him that no one thought he was the killer—although Jeek now thought that some did.

Enga Dancing Flower stood conferring with the Healer, but Jeek did not think it was about Mootak. Enga looked like she was in pain.

Chapter 21

Enga Dancing Flower did not know what to do. The tribe was dancing and she could not stand on her feet. Zhoo of Still Waters, the Healer, told her that she had some remedies for Enga to try. Sometimes they worked and sometimes they did not, she told Enga.

What are these pains? Why am I having them? Enga asked.

These are the pains that will push out the baby when it is ready. It is not now the proper time, so these pains are too early.

That worried her even more. Enga had seen babies come out before the proper time. Sometimes they were actual babies, but not alive when they emerged. Sometimes they were small beings within masses of Red and did not look much like babies at all. She was horrified by those. One of the babies that Hama lost had been like that. She did not want this for herself and Tog Flint Shaper!

Zhoo told her to sit still, on the ground, and she would return in a moment. She returned with two things, a water gourd and the small bones of the antelope they had eaten.

Drink all of this while I prepare the wet that is inside the bone.

She cracked open a thin bone. When Enga had finished drinking the water, Zhoo had her suck the wet from inside the bone. The Hamapa often did this with mammoth bones, which were much harder to break open. They had not had mammoth bones for a long time now.

Carry the rest of the bones with you, Enga Dancing Flower, and suck them often. Are you having the pains now?

Enga nodded.

Crouch like this until I tell you to get up. Zhoo demonstrated, getting onto her knees, then resting her head on her forearms which were on the ground.

Enga did it, her rump poking up. When Zhoo told her to rise, she asked if the pains were still there. They were. *I will tell you when to do this again. I hope it will help after you have done it a few more times.*

Zhoo said the best thing Enga could do was rest. It was the opinion of Zhoo that she had done too much dancing after eating too little food and walking for so many days.

If we were back in our village, Zhoo thought-spoke, with her message wrapped in the deep purple of Mother Sky on a night without Brother Moon for privacy, *I would send you to the Holy Cave. You would lie still and others would bring you food and drink.*

Will I have this baby? Enga quaked with fear. *Will the seed grow and be a healthy baby?*

Zhoo shook her head with sadness. *I do not know. If the seed stays in for the rest of the trek, that would be best. But I do not know what will happen. I hope it will.*

The Healer did not sound confident that the seed would become a baby. Enga started to quake again. Zhoo sat beside her and stroked her head and her back. Enga could not look at Zhoo. If the Healer could not tell her what would happen, she knew that no one could. She would stay as still as she could for as long as she could.

After having Enga crouch again, Zhoo left to look after Mootak again.

Her tribal brothers and sisters continued to dance and the music floated into the night air. Enga wanted to dance, to ask Dakadaga to save her baby. She had always danced to the Spirit of Mother Sky, the Most High Spirit. If she could not, would the high Spirit know she needed help?

Tog, who had been in the dance circle with Vala Golden Hair, left and came to her.

Enga Dancing Flower, we need you. The tribe needs you, our best dancer, to help get the blessings that will send us to our new home.

She shook her head and tears ran down her face.

You are in distress! Is this because I danced with Vala Golden Hair? You will not dance for the tribe because of that?

She shook her head again. *Tog Flint Shaper, the seed that we made together is in trouble. I do not know, and Zhoo of Still Waters does not know, if it will be a baby, or if it will come out too early.*

Then you must *dance!*

He jerked her to her feet and pushed her into the circle. She had trouble staying upright, so he held his arm around her waist and propelled her around. Around and around. Enga looked about for Zhoo, but she was carrying Mootak Big Heart in her arms to a place away from the dancing. She closed her eyes and moved her feet as best she could. She felt too weak even to signal to Zhoo for help. She was not dancing very well. This would not impress even a small Spirit, a Spirit of grass or leaves.

Tog Flint Shaper, I cannot dance. The Healer wants me to rest.

Tog took away his support and drew his hands away from her. *You are not concerned with the tribe. You will not dance to Dakadaga?*

I do not want to lose our precious seed. Why did Tog not understand this? *I would dance if I could. I cannot.*

Why was he being like this? Did Vala tell him that she should dance?

Tog shook his head and walked away, leaving Enga swaying precariously as the others danced around and past her. She made her way out of the circle and found a sturdy tree trunk to prop herself against. She broke another antelope bone from her satchel, which she had left on the ground, and sucked out the wetness. Her pains were worse. She watched the dancing go on without her. No one noticed her sitting in the dark and weeping, wrapping her arms around her enlarged middle where the seed grew.

Was Tog correct? Should she think of the tribe before her baby? Zhoo did not think so, but Tog did. But she could *not* dance. If the tribe perished because of her, then it would perish. There was nothing she could do to save it.

The many eyes of Dakadaga shone brightly, mocking the weak light of Brother Moon, shrunken to a narrow slice. Enga felt that her brothers and sisters were the bright, twinkling night eyes and she was dull Brother Moon. She wished very much to dance. It was what she was best at. The tribe needed her to dance. But she must save her baby. Zhoo said to rest, and she would rest as long as she could.

But what would happen at new sun when she must again start walking?

Chapter 22

When Sister Sun arose, they packed up and set out again. They walked toward the place where Sister Sun went to sleep with her mate, Brother Earth, when darkness came. They also walked toward the strange distant forms that jutted up from the edge of Brother Earth. All were curious to see what they were when they arrived at that place. There was nothing that looked like this in their old home. Enga Dancing Flower felt like she had been walking toward them for all of her life.

Enga was glad that she did not have any trouble walking. Maybe resting the night before had done her good. She had fallen asleep with her back leaning against the tree. During dark time, someone had put a skin over her and had closed up her pack, sitting beside her. She awoke rested and chewed the jerky, which was all they had again. She then broke one of the antelope bones and sucked out the inside.

Vala Golden Hair approached her, standing over her to thought-speak to her.

My little one, my Sooka, needs the wet of the bone. Give me some of that.

How could Sooka need this? She was still suckling. Enga stood up. She shook her head, snatched up her pack with the other bones inside, turned her back, and began to walk away. She did not want to converse with Vala.

But Vala persisted. *Why do you think you should get all of it?*

Enga whipped around to face her. Sooka was in her arms and smiled at Enga. The face of the baby brought tears to the eyes of Enga. Would she ever hold her own baby? *I am in danger of losing my baby. Our Healer gave me these to try to save it. You may not have them. Sooka does not need them. Sooka gets nourishment from your breasts. They have not dried up, have they?* Enga did not wait for the answer. *Even if they have, you must ask someone else to suckle Sooka.* There was only one other female who would maybe now have milk. Perhaps two. The boy of Fee Long Thrower, Whim, was one summer old and still nursing. But the baby of Fee was larger than Sooka, and older, and needed all her milk.

The other female was Hama. She had lost a baby in the last hot season before this one. It was unlikely she would still have milk, but possible.

However, Enga was sure Vala had milk. She had seen Sooka sucking the breasts of Vala every day and Sooka grew and thrived. Vala stood staring at Enga, who could feel hostility coming from her.

You suckle Sooka, Vala Golden Hair. She needs nothing else for now. I need this now. Go away from me. Do not approach me again about this. I think you want this for yourself, not for Sooka.

The pretty face of Vala turned harsh and ugly. She narrowed her eyes and sneered. *You should not address me in this manner. You will regret it.*

As Vala walked away, head held high, Enga felt a twinge of the familiar pain, but had no more of them for the rest of the day. She walked carefully, and the pains stayed away.

The distant gray shapes grew slightly larger. It could be seen that some of the tops were white, glowing in the sunlight. She thought they must be mountains, the High Places of the Saga.

When they stopped to eat and sleep, she crouched with her rear in the air as Zhoo had shown her.

Tog Flint Shaper, who had stayed away from her all day, knelt beside her. He put his head close to hers.

Enga Dancing Flower, what is this that you are doing?

She laughed at his puzzlement. *The Healer said this will help stop the pains and save the baby.*

He straightened. *So you will not dance again this dark time?*

Enga thought for a moment. She felt very good today. But if she danced, she was sure the birth pains would come back. *No I cannot. I might lose our baby.*

He rose and walked away. She saw him walking back and forth at the edge of the gathering. Maybe everyone was worried that the best dancer could not dance. But she could not.

They had stopped by a small pond which was bordered by growth, including the sturdy trees that bore the capped nuts which the bouncy, skittering little squirrels ate. Gunda and her sisters walked around the pond with their spears, looking for some of the small creatures. Jeek, who was the only male who threw a spear, went with them. The thought of a bite or two of squirrel made Enga sigh with contentment. *Fresh meat again. That would be so nice.*

Enga found a tree whose trunk had a flat side and she leaned against it, still having no pains. However, there was an ache inside when she saw Tog join Vala and Bodd Blow Striker. Sooka sat on the ground near them, still unable to move herself by either crawling or toddling. At least she could sit up, thought Enga. Such a strange child, but then she was not a full Hamapa child.

It would soon be time to dance. Enga called her birth-sister, Ung Strong Arm, over to her. *I think that it would be good to dance around this figure of Aja Hama. I believe that she is the one who guided Jeek, in his sleep, to the crossing place of the river. I think she can guide us to our new land if we dance and sing to her.*

But Enga Dancing Flower, we must give praise to Dakadaga. That is the Most High Spirit.

It will not hurt Dakadaga to also dance to this figure.

Enga did not thought-speak it, but she wondered if Dakadaga had forgotten about the Hamapa. The trek had not been easy and no one knew, even yet, if they would find a land where they could live, or if they would all die on these plains. The Hamapa could not live on the small animals they had encountered. Even the antelope took all day to trap, for just enough meat for one meal. Would Dakadaga guide them to the mammoth? She did not know. So far Dakadaga had not done this. These thoughts were tightly cloaked in her own personal soft green, the color of new leaves.

Ung was reluctant, but agreed to do what Enga wanted.

Jeek and the girls came back empty-handed and dejected. The tribe pulled out the dried jerky and ate.

Enga watched Tikihoo bite into the jerky her own tribe had given them. She liked it, but she was the only one. The others ate it because they must. Enga thought she might start to vomit if she had to eat this jerky for another full moon.

That night, there was an air of discouragement in almost everyone. When Ung proposed dancing around the figure, some shrugged and agreed. No one was enthusiastic about it.

Enga watched the dancing closely. Feet shuffled and the few spins were slow. The Hamapa were not putting their hearts into it. This was not the way to win the favor of the gods. The song of Lakala was not being sung to Aja Hama, but to Dakadaga, the Spirit who had not helped them. Enga wanted her to sing to many Spirits. She wanted to dance to many, to Leela, Spirit of the Hunt; to Aysha, Spirit of Birthing; to Ohla, Spirit of Healing, and to others. Some of these, the birthing Spirit and the healing one, Enga wanted for herself. But she could not dance for herself. Now, she could not dance at all.

The dispirited dancing ended, trailing off into almost nothing. Those not still dancing prepared to sleep.

Then Enga caught sight of Tog and Vala together. They were not dancing. Vala had laid out her sleeping skin and Tog was on it with her and Sooka. Bodd Blow Striker had left the dance also and was pacing in the darkness, beyond the light, as he had done in the past.

Enga sent up her own supplication to Puka, Spirit of Strife. She fervently wanted the strife between her and her mate to end.

The thoughts of her brothers and sisters intruded. Many of them were unsettled because they did not know who had killed Panan

One Eye. Had their minds changed, or had they given their thoughts falsely, as she had?

Hapa publicly suggested that someone keep watch, maybe two people, each for half of dark time. All were tired from walking all day and none volunteered. Enga thought it was a good idea, but could see why no one wanted to stay up half the night and lose so much sleep. It would be hard to make progress the next day if some were too tired to keep up.

Hapa grew angry that no one would help keep watch. He stomped off, toward the pond, and stood looking across it. She thought he must be worried about the killer among them, since they had never kept watch on this trek. But she could not read his thoughts.

Enga felt a thought coming to her from Hapa. *Enga Dancing Flower, do you remember that we are trying to find out who killed our Elder? Have you found out anything?*

She had not forgotten, but had had much concern for losing the baby. She answered him. *I have tried, but I have not learned anything. I will try some more tonight.* And she would. She would stay awake as long as she could, listening in on the thoughts of others. Maybe it was more convenient for her to have Tog with Vala. But just for now. She wanted him to come back soon. The space beside her was cold.

Chapter 23

"Music appears to mimic some of the features of language and to convey some of the same emotions...but far more than language, music taps into primitive brain structures involved with motivation, reward, and emotion."

—*This Is Your Brain on Music*
by Daniel J. Levitin, p. 191

Enga Dancing Flower found that she could not stay awake long. She bedded down near Fee Long Thrower, her mate Bahg Swiftfeet, and their son. Fee and Bahg Swiftfeet sent some thoughts back and forth, not shielded from Enga, or from anyone. They were both weary of the jerky and hoped to reach the final destination soon. They were not thinking any dark thoughts, not thinking about who killed Panan One Eye.

Ongu Small One and her mate Sannum Straight Hair were near, with their three sons, including Mootak Big Heart. Their main concern was Mootak, that he had not fully recovered yet from seeing the white figure with the rock, or maybe not recovered from the calming herbs. They did not think Mootak killed Panan, but did not suspect anyone else.

The Healer, Zhoo of Still Waters, was already asleep beside her sons, Teek Bearclaw and young Jeek. Teek and Jeek lay awake and discussed how to find and track game in this place, so different from their home. They did not think about the killer.

None of these kept secret dark thoughts where Enga could discover them.

She fell asleep before she could touch the minds of any others. Maybe Hapa would be more successful.

A wave of hostility jolted Enga wide awake. She sat up, alarmed. Mootak and Ongu, his birth-mother, stood confronting Hapa, who had come back from gazing across the water. Enga could not catch the thoughts, but their anger flowed flaming bright to Hapa.

Hapa turned his head when Enga sat up. Then others, also disturbed, awoke. Some stood and walked over to the three. The mate of Ongu, Sannum, sat with their other two offspring, but frowned at Hapa.

Finally, Hama came to them. *What is this dissention? Why are all of you not sleeping and preparing for a long walk?*

Ongu Small One crossed her arms before her and answered Hama. *Hapa is invading our minds. He is looking for the killer of Panan One Eye. He thinks Sannum Straight Hair, Mootak Big Heart, or I—Ongu Small One—lifted the rock that killed him.*

Hapa held up his palms. *I do not think this, Ongu Small One.*

She whirled on him, her long braid swinging with her rage. *Then why are you in our minds? Why would you do this if you did not think so?*

Enga could see what the problem was. Hapa was not born in the Hamapa tribe. He came from another tribe to mate with Roh Lion Hunter when he was an adult, Donik Tree Trunk—the small and the tall coming together. Since he was not closely related to everyone in the tribe, his mind gropings were clumsy. Enga knew she could flit in and out of the thoughts of her brothers and sisters and not be detected. She was adopted into the tribe, that was true, but she was so young when she came to the Hamapa, that she and her sister, Ung Strong Arm, easily learned all their ways.

Let us hold a council, Ongu thought-spoke.

Now? In the deepest of dark time? Hama snorted. *No, we will not do this thing. Everyone, lie down and sleep. We will be on our way very soon.*

All lay down as Hama had commanded, but not many slept.

As Sister Sun showed the first curve of her face, shooting out bright rays that leaped into Mother Sky, Hama called for all to arise and get ready to walk.

Ongu and Sannum blocked her way and stood with their arms folded across their chests. Cabat the Thick came to stand beside them. The life flow inside Enga turned cold. A confrontation right now could not be a good thing.

We shall have a council now, since you would not have one in dark time, Hama. The thought-speak of Cabat was harsh and commanding. *There is a proposal to be considered.*

Hama frowned, but stood beside them and beckoned everyone to circle around them. *What is this proposal?*

We must consider banishing our Elder, our Hapa. Ongu stated this, her face defiant and stony.

A collective gasp was audible. Enga was as confused as she was worried. Banish an Elder? How could anyone think of such a thing?

Hama was the only one who remained calm, as befitted her station as their Most High Leader. *What is the reason for this request? This very odd request.*

Ongu looked to her mate and he took over. Sannum gestured toward Hapa as he thought-spoke. *This one, our own Elder, our Most High Male, has shown that we cannot trust him. He is invading our minds to steal our private thoughts.*

Enga knew that Hapa could not steal their private thoughts, although Sannum might think he could. He could barely see into their minds. Too late, she wished she had warned him to take much care and not to be obvious in his probings. Now his clumsiness would make it hard for her to do her own search. Everyone would be guarding their thoughts, clamping them down tight.

Hama drew her brows together and answered with a sternness that crackled in the mind of Enga. *We will not banish an Elder. It is not done. Maybe we should think of banishing the one who killed Panan One Eye.* Hama gave a hard look at Ongu, then at Sannum.

They both took a step back, away from her, shock on their faces.

So, Enga thought, no one actually believes that a Spirit killed Panan. Everyone gave a false opinion. It was for the good of the tribe, but maybe it was not the right thing to do.

Ongu thought-spoke first. *You think I, Ongu Small One, slew Panan One Eye? Or that my mate did this terrible thing?*

Hama turned her gaze upon their birth-son, the new Storyteller, Mootak Big Heart. *There was only one person on that side of the river with Panan One Eye.*

Now Cabat sliced his hands through the air with anger. *It has never been done, but that does not mean it can never happen. We could banish both our Most High Female and our Most High Male.*

Chaos ensued. Everyone shouted their thoughts. The air rippled with bright red fury, with vivid orange rage, and with sickening agitation. Enga could almost see strands of tension straining them all. She turned her face toward Mother Sky, where Sister Sun was now halfway up. She sent her silent supplication to Dakadaga.

A sweet sound of song cut through the turmoil. Lakala Rippling Water raised her arms high and sang an entreaty to Puka, the Spirit of Strife. She sang for harmony. The Gata male, Fall Cape Maker, ran for the flute and joined her.

The brow of Enga eased. Her muscles relaxed. She bowed her head and stood to take a few shuffling dance steps. Ung Strong Arm joined her, then Fee and Zhoo, then some of the males. Soon most of them were circling the Singer and their new flute player. Enga dropped out, afraid for the seed she carried, but the flow of music and dance calmed the tribe, as it always did. The love for music and dance, for rhythm and pleasing sound, ran deep in the Hamapa. They had made music and had danced as far back as their Sagas went.

The matter was not settled. No one knew who had killed Panan. But they were now able to gnaw a bit of jerky, pack up, and move on. Sister Sun shone at their backs, casting long shadows across the flat prairie. Drops of dew glistened on the long grasses. Small animals and insects rustled in the growth. And the Hamapa trudged on, an uneasy truce hovering above them like the menace of a storm cloud. Enga continued to try to detect the thoughts of a killer, but could not.

At dark time, when most were asleep, Enga lay awake, troubled. She caught some stray thoughts and strained to understand them.

What if someone found out? What if Hama finds out?

Those two came through clearly and she concentrated harder. A dark shape walked back and forth at the edge of the place where they slept. The person was a mere shadow, but the shape was too tall to be anyone but Hapa. What secret was he holding? Enga turned her head toward him and opened her mind all the way.

Hapa hung his head for a few moments, then raised it and walked back to lie beside Hama. Enga would keep track of his thoughts and try to find out what he was holding in his mind. It must have been something he had done. Something he wished he had not done.

They plodded on, growing more and more weary of the trek, through rain showers, punishing heat, and a few downpours that had them running for the nearest trees to seek shelter. They came to no more wide rivers, only narrow streams that were easily crossed. Yet, each time they encountered one, all minds turned to the terrible crossing and the death of their Storyteller. Most nights they bedded down without dancing, singing, or any Saga or council. It was understood that they must keep going, no matter what else happened.

At last they approached the gray shapes. They had loomed larger and more distinct every day until it could be seen that they were huge rock masses, mountains, too high to go over. They stretched as far one way as the next. The tribe could not go around them, either.

Even more discouraged than they had been, they halted and camped for several suns.

That is when it happened.

Chapter 24

"Dr. Marcia Ponce de León and Prof. Christoph Zollikofer from the Anthropological Institute of the University of Zurich examined the birth and the brain development of a newborn Neanderthal baby from the Mezmaiskaya Cave in the Crimea. That Neanderthal child, which died shortly after it was born, was evidently buried with such care that it was able to be recovered in good condition from the cave sediments of the Ice Age after resting for approximately 40,000 years... They discovered that the brain at the time of birth was of exactly the same size as a typical human newborn... However, the skeleton was considerably more robustly formed than that of a modern human newborn. ...for the Neanderthals, the birth was probably about as difficult as it is for our own race."

—from: University of Zurich. "Childbirth Was Already Difficult For Neanderthals."
ScienceDaily, 9 September 2008.
<www.sciencedaily.com/releases/
2008/09/080908203013.htm>

The pains of Enga Dancing Flower pierced her body, then subsided, then started up again many times. Now that everyone had quit walking for a few suns, she could no longer ignore the agonizing spasms. They were getting worse.

For some time, the torture of watching Tog Flint Shaper with Vala Golden Hair every sun time and every dark time had covered up any other pain she might have. It also hurt her that he seemed to love little Sooka so much, when Enga was carrying the seed he has planted. Did he not care about his own seed?

Now she could no longer ignore the rhythmic clenchings in her gut. She cried out at dark time after the tribe had been stopped by the mountains for a few suns, not knowing how to move on. Zhoo of Still Waters ran to her. She held Enga in the head down position and gave her even more bones to suck from her own stash. In-between crouching with her rear in the air, she lay still and drank water, as Zhoo told her to do.

Complete darkness approached.

None of it helped.

My dear Enga Dancing Flower. Zhoo sat beside her and wiped the sweat from her forehead with her own clothing. *You have eaten too little. You have walked too much. And you have danced too hard. There is nothing I can do to help you and the small seed.*

Enga called out for her birth-sister. Ung Strong Arm came running and knelt beside Enga. *What can I do?* she asked Enga and Zhoo.

Zhoo shook her head.

Stay with me, Enga thought-spoke.

I will stay with you as you stayed with me when my leg was injured by the peccary on the hunt and my Red poured out onto the ground.

The very clear image of that time made the pains of Enga worse. But she knew Ung would stay with her. The mate of Ung, Lakala Rippling Water, also drew near.

Zhoo thought-spoke. *I wish we had our Cave. I would take you there to go through your ordeal. This is not right that you should go through this travail with the whole tribe watching.*

Enga raised her head slightly. It did seem that everyone was paying attention, waiting for her to lose the baby. When she looked around, all turned away and busied themselves. If they had possessed the ears of cats, however, she knew those ears would be swiveling in her direction. She closed her eyes and submerged herself in a vision of the Holy Cave on the Sacred Hill. It was cool inside, and quiet, and private. She and Zhoo and Ung were the only ones in the Cave. She was on a thick pallet of dried grasses and cushioned by many soft animal skins, deer and bear.

She heard night insects whirring, and the distant hoot of an owl, and those sounds further helped her to envision being back home in the comfortable Cave.

When Zhoo stroked her forehead, Enga smiled, happy to be back in the Cave, the place where she had gone with the older women when she got her first Red Flow. The place where she had had her First Coupling with Tog. He was there with her. He caressed her face, her body. She stroked his strong, broad back. Their eyes looked deep into each other. And now she was in the Holy Cave having their child. She smiled again, until a stabbing pain caused her to grunt and curl up in agony. She returned to what was happening.

She was not having the baby. She was losing the baby.

After the gush of Red had passed, Enga was carried away from that spot to recover. She lay exhausted while Brother Moon followed his silent path across Mother Sky. One by one, her brothers and sisters came to her. They offered a sympathetic nod, or a pat on her shoulder. Some sat with her for a while, hushed and somber.

Enga fell asleep, waking up several times and falling asleep again. There was always someone with her. Halfway through the dark time, she raised herself on an elbow and looked for what was left of her baby. The pile was not far away. It glistened darkly in the light from the sky. Her baby. She realized tears were falling from her eyes, dropping onto the ground. She dropped off her elbow, still drained and shattered.

No one got up at first light. They lingered, lying until Hama gave the signal to arise.

Finally Hama stood up. She sent a message to everyone. *We have not walked for several days. We do not walk today, either. We will have a ritual for the seed of Enga Dancing Flower and Tog Flint Shaper.*

When Enga heard his name in the thought-speak, she looked around for Tog. Had he come to be beside her in the dark time? She did not know. She could ask Ung or Zhoo, but she did not want to find out that he had not been there, so she kept that question to herself.

Now he came forward, without Vala Golden Hair or Sooka. He squatted next to Enga. She looked away from him, keeping her gaze upon Hama.

That day the tribe mourned the unnamed baby. There were no flower petals to scatter in the path, so they gathered colorful leaves from beneath the nearby trees. Some were scarlet and orange, the hues of the streaks Sister Sun sent across Mother Sky as she went to sleep every night with her mate, Brother Earth.

The pile of Red, which contained the tiny incomplete body, was put onto a remnant of mammoth hide by Hapa. He signaled to Tog and the two of them carried the small form away, followed by the tribe. The children of Hama and of Ongu Small One scattered the leaves before them as they went. Akkal Firetender had scouted earlier and had found a rock outcropping near a small pond. It was not large, but neither was the body. It was out of sight from where they were camped.

Ung and Lakala supported Enga as she trailed behind the rest to the spot where her dead baby was laid. She was too weak to stand on her own.

Scavengers would come for the tiny body and it would be returned to Brother Earth in that way. There was no need to smear fat on the body so that it would go quickly. The Red would attract animals in its place.

After Hapa and Tog unwrapped and placed the body on the rock, the children scattered the rest of the colored leaves onto it. Each one spoke thoughts to the child who had never lived. Then they all returned to where they had been. No one wanted to stay at the rock and see what happened next. The doings of Brother Earth when he worked with Gongor, the Spirit of Death, were best left unseen.

As dark time gathered, the tribe came to Enga one at a time. Some gave her words of comfort, others touched her on the shoulder or the head. Each time, Enga felt more and more sobs catching in her throat, until she wailed out loud.

She quieted only when Hapa came to her, and only because of her intense interest in what he was hiding. She kept sobbing a bit, not calmed or consoled, but remembering she had not yet found out what he had worried about when she had seen him pacing at dark time, she tried to stay receptive to his thoughts.

Our dear Enga Dancing Flower, we are so sorry you lost the baby.

That is what many of them had said. She thanked him, looking deep into his mind. It was different enough that she could not see clearly into it. Most of his thoughts were murky.

At the next new sun, Hama called a council. All agreed they could stay in this place no longer. They must move, but they could not move past the mountains.

We must proceed in the direction away from the Guiding Bear of Mother Sky. Hama pointed in the direction where the Guiding Bear could be seen at dark time. *If we go toward it, we will be going toward a colder place. There will be no mammoth there.*

Cabat the Thick interjected. *Do we know there will be mammoth in the other direction?*

Hama answered. *It does not matter what we know. We must hope. That is all we can do.*

Hapa backed her up, as did most of the tribe. Enga agreed also. They must go toward a warmer clime. That is where the mammoth had fled toward.

They had to hope they would find mammoth before Cold Season commenced. All they had now were a bit more of the hard, unpalatable jerky, and hope.

Chapter 25

"During the Wisconsin glaciation... Most of the state was covered by montane coniferous forest, composed of Douglas Fir (*Pseudotsuga mensiesii*), Southwestern White Pine (*Pinus strobiformis*), and White Fir (*Abies concolor*).

— *New Mexico Vegetation*: past, present, and future
by William A. Dick-Peddie

"The largest glyptodont that roamed North America, *Glyptotherium arizonae*, weighed at least 1 ton. It measured 10 feet (3 meters) long, and 4.5 feet (1.5 meters) tall... [It] retreated south to Mexico and then returned to the United States in the Rancholabrean Land Mammal Age, only to become extinct everywhere by 10,000 years ago."

— *Ice Age Mammals* by Ian M. Lange, p. 73

Jeek thought they had been walking for about one-quarter of the cycle of a moon, the number of days on one hand, plus two. The breath of Mother Sky got warmer every day, it seemed. They were now heading away from the Guiding Bear, which they could only see at dark time, of course. They had the mountains on one side to guide them in addition to the Guiding Bear.

The terrain also changed. When they came to a land covered with thick pines, Jeek enjoyed the shade. Sister Sun seemed to grow brighter and bigger as they traveled.

He knew that others were keeping an eye on Enga Dancing Flower, but he did also. He would not be able to bear it if any more terrible things happened to her. Her mate, Tog Flint Shaper, sometimes stayed with her, but sometimes with Vala Golden Hair. Jeek could not understand why anyone would leave Enga, ever. Even when Tog left her, there were no harsh vibrations he could pick up. Did Enga want him to visit Vala? He wished he were older so he could understand some things.

The kinds of animals he saw changed as they progressed, but there were familiar ones also. They had not seen mammoth yet, but one of the hunting females had spotted a large herd of bison, far in the distance. The mouth of Jeek dripped at the thought of fresh meat. There had been bison where they used to live, but they had always preferred mammoth. The meat from such a large animal lasted a long time after it was smoked, and the watering hole where those mammoth had gathered had been a perfect distance away. There would be so much to learn in the new place.

During one of the traveling days, Hama decided to stop early since everyone was weary and spirits were low. As the tribe found shady places to lean against tree trunks or to lie on skins spread over soft beds of pine needles, Jeek stood watching Gunda dribble water into the mouths of her small sisters. He was tired, but too restless to lie and nap.

When Gunda looked up at him, he sent her a thought. *Would you like to climb the nearest rock with me?*

He grinned when she nodded. They started for the bluff that was most near. It was not very high and Jeek thought they could get to the top and return before dark time.

They came upon Tikihoo, who had left the group and was looking up at the hill. She raised her eyebrows in question and pointed up to the rocky place.

Jeek and Gunda pointed to themselves and the bluff, trying to tell her they were going up. When Tikihoo pointed to her own chest, then drew a circle including the three of them, they understood that she wanted to go with them. Jeek did not know why she wanted to go, but he could sense fear radiating from her. Tikihoo looked back at the tribe as they climbed, like she wanted to get away from someone. He wished, not for the first time, that he could communicate with her.

About halfway up, Gunda and Jeek were glad Tikihoo was with them. She was the only one who had brought along a water gourd. They all three drank a few sips, wanting to save some for the rest of the climb, and for the descent. The slope was not steep, but there were plants with sharp spines growing among others with soft leaves, sometimes hidden, so that they had to be careful not to get stuck. Sister Sun smiled on them, but Jeek wished Mother Sky would put on some thick cloud garments. She seldom did lately. Instead, she arched above them in the blue of deep water at sunrise when the water held not a ripple or a current.

When they reached the top, the three looked toward the place Sister Sun rose from in the mornings, away from the tall mountains behind them. The plains stretched far away, etched with small streams that were bordered by a few trees.

Why did you want to go up here? Gunda asked Jeek.

To see what is ahead of us. And anything else that— He stopped his thought when he spotted a cloud of dust rising from the flat land. *Do you see that? What do you think it is?*

Gunda squinted to see anything at such a distance. Tikihoo pointed and jumped up and down, smiling. She was making her mouth noises, but Jeek did not understand them now more than he ever did. "Gadoo, gadoo!" She made other noises too, but this was the one she kept repeating.

The cloud was coming toward them. After a few moments, Jeek could make out animals, running in a herd, going fast.

Horses! Gunda thought-spoke.

Jeek had never seen them, but had received pictures of them during Sagas.

Then Jeek saw the beautiful slender legs and flying manes and tails of the ones in the lead. He thought that "gadoo" must mean horse or horses. The herd galloped ever more close. There was a stream between them and the animals. Maybe they were coming to water there.

All three scrambled down the slope as fast as they could. Jeek wanted to alert the tribe. Maybe they could spear one and have fresh meat. But, by the time they reached the bottom, the horses had galloped into the distance. The herd had run toward the stream, but had veered before reaching it and had run back the way they came, probably frightened off by the smell of the Hamapa.

Jeek saw the beautiful animals in his mind for many days after that.

* * *

Enga Dancing Flower was despondent much of the time about losing the baby. But one thing made her happy. Tog Flint Shaper was helping her to examine the minds of the tribe. The three of them agreed that Hapa should not do it any more. Some nights Tog would go over to Vala Golden Hair so he could get close to those not near Enga and observe them.

What made Enga the most glad was that Tog told her he did not want to mate with Vala, or to be around her often. He felt bad for Sooka, and Enga did also, since Vala did not take the kind of care of the infant that Enga or Tog would. It was true, Sooka was more slow to do everything than normal, but she was a joyful little girl, easy to manage if someone paid attention to her. Vala grew very impatient and sometimes would stalk off and leave the baby sitting on the ground, alone and crying.

Enga learned that, much as Tog liked Sooka, though, he no longer liked being around Vala. Vala never thought good thoughts about anyone. She only schemed about what others could do for her. He told Enga that he was amazed that Vala was the birth-sister of Hama and birth-daughter of the most recent Hama. Her seed giver, Kokat One Ear, who was long dead, had been a kind and generous brother, although her birth-mother, the late Hama, had not been a nice person.

Still, neither Enga nor Tog caught any hints of dark, stray thoughts about the death of Panan One Eye.

Enga continued to comfort Tikihoo, who was, she thought, mourning the loss of Panan. He was the reason she had left her own tribe and joined them. If Enga could understand the sounds of Tikihoo, she thought she might find out that the Hooden female wished she had never left her people to join the Hamapa.

Enga wondered about one thing that Tikihoo did. She interacted, as well as she could, with most of the tribe members. But she avoided Vala Golden Hair. She helped out when she could, letting Enga lean on her when she felt weak, and helping the older members set up their sleeping skins at dark time. But she would not help take care of Sooka.

One time Enga had the infant and needed to step away to squat and relieve herself of her waste. Tikihoo was near. She had been helping Enga carry her pack. But when Enga handed Sooka to Tikihoo, the Hooden backed away, putting her arms out, showing her palms and shaking her head. She would not even touch little Sooka.

When Vala came near Tikihoo she trembled and Enga was sure she was frightened of Vala. Most of the tribe did not like Vala. It would be surprising if Tikihoo liked her.

Enga was glad that Fall Cape Maker was becoming friends with Tikihoo. They had mated several times and slept together most nights.

While walking one day, the tribe encountered a strange animal they had not seen before. It had a face rather like a beaver, but without the protruding teeth. It may have had a similar body, but that could not be seen beneath the hard-looking covering over all of it, including a tail that looked like it would do damage. The creature stood in their path, looking at them from small, hard eyes. Pointed ears poked up beside the hard, bumpy head cover.

Enga saw Jeek staring and peeked inside his mind while he was occupied. Jeek very much wanted to touch it to see what the shell felt like, but was intimidated.

Enga also took a few quick glimpses into the thoughts of Fall and Teek, who had been stranded with Panan. No shadows lurked. She even ventured into the mind of Hapa, but it was different enough that she still could not read the edges of it, where dark thoughts would be hidden.

Her attention went back to the animal. The beast was gigantic. It was as tall as one Hamapa and the length was that of two Hamapas. It took steps toward them on clawed feet that stuck out beneath the shell. The tribe moved toward it as a group, all wanting to poke it and feel it.

Tikihoo tugged at Enga and pulled, then she tried to pull Jeek away. She seemed greatly alarmed and waved her arms to get them to move away.

Enga was puzzled. The beast looked too large and heavy to move fast. She pointed at the animal, then turned her palm down with her fingers extended to make it look like the thing. She moved her fingers slowly and simulated plodding. Tikihoo shook her head. She pointed at it, then glanced one palm off the other, shooting one hand out to demonstrate that it was quick, Enga thought.

The others gave in and moved away. But Enga wondered how much meat was beneath that shell, and if there was any way to get to it.

One sun later, Bahg Swiftfeet and Tog Flint Shaper climbed a rocky outcrop to see what lay ahead. Soon they both sent urgent messages for them to all come up to the top. Enga, helped by Tikihoo, made her way up the steep, jagged climb and, when they were all there, followed the gaze of Bahg and Tog. In the distance, on a flat plain, two gigantic beasts with shells, like the one they had encountered, stood facing each other. The strange beasts swayed their heads back and forth and swished their hard tails. Then, almost too quickly for them to see, one pivoted and whacked the other in the neck with its tail. As fast as a flash of lightning, the attacker was far across the plain. The injured animal sank to the ground, Red pouring from its neck.

Enga looked at Tikihoo with her eyes and mouth wide open with amazement. Tikihoo pursed her lips and nodded. Enga wished she could ask Tikihoo how to slay these animals and whether the meat was good. But then she remembered that the awful-tasting jerky came from her tribe. If Tikihoo liked to eat them, Enga might not.

They scurried down, ready to continue, since their path would not take them near the battle they had just seen.

A small band of tall, thin males blocked their way. They stood frowning, arms folded across their chests.

Chapter 26

The Hamapa sent mental messages to each other that these were Tall Ones, like the male who had given the seed for little Sooka. That one, called Stitcher, had left the tribe before the child was born, so Sooka was the only one of them with the Hamapa now. Enga knew they would not be able to communicate with these any better than they could the Hooden. She could not tell if they were curious or hostile. The smell of their clothing was different, but their hair and bodies reminded her very much of Stitcher. In fact, Sooka bore a trace of the same odor. Maybe they smelled this way because they ate different foods, or because of the animals whose skins they wore. It was more likely that their bodies just smelled different, though.

The hides they wore resembled those of the galloping herd of horses they had spotted on their way to this place. At the same time, they were similar to Stitcher and Sooka, and yet different.

Tikihoo stepped up to them, showing no fear. She started spouting sounds that meant nothing to the Hamapa. The most tall one shook his head. The Hooden tried again and this time he smiled and answered with the same nonsense sounds.

Tikihoo could talk to the Tall Ones with sounds! That was wonderful. Enga Dancing Flower, along with the whole tribe, followed the exchange closely, not understanding any of the sounds. Tikihoo waved an arm at the Hamapa behind her, then gestured in the direction they had come from. She also indicated where they were trying to go.

Then she seemed puzzled at how to continue. She tried a few sounds, but the Tall Ones did not comprehend, shaking their heads again. Tikihoo motioned for Enga to come forward. She touched the mammoth skin garment Enga wore. Then she seemed to describe the animal it had come from, holding her arms out and looking up to indicate the size and drawing the tusks of the mammoth coming from her own mouth into the air.

The most tall one came next to Enga and also touched her mammoth skin. That seemed to convince him. He nodded at Enga and at Tikihoo.

Next, Tikihoo asked some questions. They answered, pointing in the direction the Hamapa had been heading.

Enga studied the one who acted as leader. She saw similarities between him and Sooka. Maybe Stitcher had been related to these. Their garments were held together with fine thread, stitched so that it held the edges of their garments together. That was the art that Stitcher knew also. Or maybe it was common to Tall Ones. Or maybe this was the tribe that had cast him out.

When they were finished, the Tall Ones stood aside and the Hamapa continued on their way. Tikihoo stopped them when the Tall Ones were out of sight. She touched the skin Enga wore one more time and pointed at Sister Sun. She held up all the fingers on one hand.

The Hamapa all understood that she was telling them how many suns they needed to go to reach the mammoth. Enga felt like stopping for a dance immediately, but Sister Sun was still high and they could travel much more before dark time. Joyful thoughts flew back and forth, thoughts of a big kill, plenty to eat, new clothing and new skins for their dwellings. The ones they had dragged and carried and worn for so long were thin and ragged now.

The large skin that held the spears and tools had holes in it. When two spears fell out, it had been replaced by the extra hide that Hapa had wanted to bring. Panan One Eye had argued against doing that, but when it came about that the idea of Hapa was a good one, he had not mentioned the argument.

There was an air of happiness when they camped at the end of the sun time. They knew they would soon see the mammoth herds.

Enga saw Tikihoo gesturing and nodding with Fall Cape Maker. Jeek was standing nearby. They seemed to be communicating. Tikihoo was agitated, worried looking, in spite of the happy news they had gotten through her that day. Enga wondered what was wrong. Jeek joined them and looked like he tried to follow the exchange, but looked puzzled by the whole thing.

Enga bedded down with Tog Flint Shaper at her side, more content than she had been in some time. She had felt much more strong today and had walked the whole way without assistance. For that she was glad. She sent a private message of thanks to Dakadaga before she fell asleep. She also included Aja Hama in her gratitude, rubbing her thumb over the belly of the carving, then putting it safely back inside her pouch.

Tog threw his strong arm across her and she drifted into a deep, happy sleep.

At first sun, she felt a disturbance in the tranquility that had prevailed last night. When she sat up, Tog was gone from her side. She spotted him running toward the foot of a rock bluff along with several other males. The pictures they were projecting were distressing.

She had to run after them to see for herself, though she could not yet run at her most quick speed. Soon the whole tribe was gathered. Enga pushed through her brothers and sisters to see what they all looked at. No one was transmitting thought pictures.

Lying on the ground beneath the cliff was a broken body, the legs and arm splayed out, one leg snapped into two pieces. It was hard to tell who it was, the head was so thoroughly smashed. But, from the darkness of the skin, it was obvious that this was Tikihoo. This body was that of the Hooden.

Enga looked up. She had to have fallen from the top of the cliff. But what would she have been doing up there?

Fall and Jeek stood together and it looked like they were exchanging private thoughts.

* * *

Jeek had seen a lot of terrible things happen to his tribemates. This was one of the worst. She was not a tribemate yet. She would eventually have become one, he was sure, but at this time she was a Hooden who was travelling with them. She had no role in the tribe and no mate except maybe Fall Cape Maker. It had once seemed she would be the mate of Panan One Eye, before he had been killed. By a ghost, if one believed what Mootak Big Heart related.

He thought hard, scrunching his eyes closed and picturing her gestures at the last dark time to him and to Fall Cape Maker. She had been trying to convey something to them, but neither had understood her actions. Had she thought she was in danger from someone and tried to tell them?

When he felt a finger poke his arm, he jumped, eyes wide open now. It was only Fall Cape Maker.

What was she trying to tell us? Fall thought-spoke in a private color, asking the same question Jeek had been asking himself.

Jeek shook his head. He did not know. *Can we go over all of her actions and try to tell what she was upset about?*

We can try. But I did not understand then. I may not ever.

Jeek pondered how they could do this. He suspected that whatever she was afraid of, or whatever person she was afraid of, had lured her up that cliff and pushed her off. *Let us climb to the top and see if we can tell what happened up there.*

Do you think that is wise? If someone pushed her and the one who killed her sees us, we will be in danger.

Jeek thought-spoke, *It could be that she climbed up there by herself and fell. It could be that her people worship high places.*

Jeek knew there were Sagas about that, even about people like the Hamapa who considered high places sacred. Where was Mootak Big Heart? He must ask him about that. The Hooden were not people like the Hamapa, but they were more alike them than some. The Tall Ones and the fierce little Mikino were more different.

He called Mootak over to join him and Fall.

Mootak Big Heart, could you recite part of a Saga about holy high places? About the ones who held them sacred? Jeek asked.

Do you think Tikihoo was like that? Mootak thought-spoke. *Did she go up there to be near her Spirits, and then get too close to the edge and fall over?*

We do not know, Fall answered. *But maybe hearing the details of a Saga of High Places will help us understand if that is what happened.*

Mootak nodded. He raised his face to Mother Sky and closed his eyes, going through the Sagas in his mind. *There is a Saga of creation from Mother Sky. It says she sent bright thunderbolts shooting down until Brother Earth was born from them. Is that what you were thinking of?*

Jeek shook his head. *Are there other Sagas about the high places of Brother Earth?*

There is the Saga of the Creation of High Places. Mootak started to recite. *In the most early times Brother Earth lay flat. He had no rivers. He had no low places and no high places. Sister Sun was not interested in him and she stayed with Mother Sky all of the time. She never came down to Brother Earth to be with him. Then Mother Sky got tired of looking at Brother Earth, all flat. She blew her hottest breath, then her coldest breath. Brother Earth got frightened and large hills erupted, spewing hot, melted rocks toward Mother Sky and Sister Sun. Sister Sun rejoiced. She liked the hot melted rocks. They were scorching, searing hot, like her.*

She began to come closer to Brother Earth to see the places where Brother Earth spit out the melted rocks. That is when she began to sleep with him and there became sun time and dark time.

Over a long, long period, the places where the melted rock poured forth became cool and became high places. Some were so cold that white snow collected on their tops.

Mootak fell silent. Jeek felt blessed. He had just heard a Saga, given for him and Fall only. He thanked Mootak for this and Mootak, looking like he wanted to rest, walked away.

I do not know how this Saga can help us understand what happened to Tikihoo, Jeek.

Jeek agreed. *We should go up there to see if we can figure out what happened, but we should not let anyone see us.*

They wandered away from the group, still gathered around the broken body, giving it all their attention. The pair went around the jagged cliff until they were on another side, out of sight, and began to climb.

Chapter 27

"The living California Condor and the Pleistocene condors, especially the condor represented in the Rancho La Brea deposits, have either been considered as separate species (*G. californianus* and *G. amplus*) or the Pleistocene form has been considered a temporal subspecies of *G. californianus*. The primary difference...was size, the Pleistocene form being larger... Although the distribution of modern condors is limited to California and introductions into Arizona and Nevada, past distribution of condors apparently was far greater, with the birds withstanding Pleistocene climatic conditions as far east and north as the state of New York (Steadman and Miller 1987)."

—from: *Gymnogyps* Lesson 1842—
California/Rancho La Brea Condor,
https://www.utep.edu/leb/pleistNM/
taxaAves/Gymnogypscalifornianus.htm

Enga Dancing Flower noticed when Jeek and Fall Cape Maker left the group. She did not call attention to it because she guessed what they were doing. They were going to climb up to see if they could tell what had happened up there to cause Tikihoo to fall. She hooked into the thought-stream between the two, which was not shielded with care, to confirm her guess. They probably felt no need for a good shield since everyone was concentrating on the body of Tikihoo and wondering what had happened to her.

Enga hoped they would find something. It was obvious to her that someone had killed Tikihoo. That meant they traveled either with a person who could kill two people and mask such deeds from everyone, or with two such people. Should they keep traveling with such persons? Or should they stop and figure out who these beings were?

That was for the Elders to say, but maybe a council should be held. It would be good to hear from each person. Hama and the Elders could try to determine who any killers were. Enga had not gotten any answers in trying to search the minds of her tribemates. Hapa had learned nothing. Even Tog Flint Shaper, who was trying the same as Enga, to see into all the minds, had not found out anything.

Maybe Jeek and Fall would see something on top of the cliff that would give them information, would let them know who had been up there with her. In the mind of Enga was the certain thought that someone had pushed her. She did not know why she was certain, but she was.

Hama touched her thoughts. *Enga Dancing Flower, do you know anything about the death of Tikihoo?*

Enga sent back her answer, that she knew nothing.

Will you ask your brothers and sisters what they were doing during dark time? Maybe an answer that is given will be false and you will be able to find the slayer of Tikihoo.

So Hama also believed Tikihoo was killed. That was interesting. *I will try to do this, my Hama.* It was also interesting that Hapa must not have shared with Hama the project he and Enga were working on.

She smiled a slow, slight smile. Now she had permission from the Most High Leader to work in the open to find out the truth. *As soon as Tikihoo is given back to Brother Earth, I shall start.*

Hama agreed with that plan.

Since the poor dead female was not of the tribe, Enga wondered what would happen to her body.

Her question was answered when Hama thought-spoke to everyone a few moments later. *The Hooden female will remain here, where her life left her. We will continue our trek as soon as everyone is ready to go.*

Enga frowned, facing away from Hama. That did not seem fitting. No, the Hooden was not a Hamapa, but she was still a person. A shadow passed over them and she looked up to see the black and white underside feathers on the wings of a flesh-eating bird. Many of them circled above, blocking out the rays of Sister Sun as they cast their large shadows on the small group of beings. Tikihoo would not remain undisturbed for very long after they left. She hoped that the birds would not swoop down before they were out of sight.

She sent an urgent message to Jeek that he and Fall should come back because the tribe was about to leave. She sensed Vala Golden Hair studying her and turned to see if Vala wanted anything from her. She could not read the expression on the face of Vala and could not read a single thought from her mind either. She was glad that her message to Jeek and Fall had been cloaked well.

As soon as they were underway, she would start asking the questions as Hama had requested. Should she deal with Vala first or last?

Jeek and Fall came trotting into sight. Jeek let her know they had not been able to reach the top. An easier path to the top lay within sight of everyone, but they did not want to be seen, so they had not taken it. The other, more difficult way, would have taken much time.

That told Enga that Tikihoo and the other person had probably gone up the rocks at dark time. If they had gone up after Sister Sun rose from lying with Brother Earth, someone would have seen them. Maybe everyone.

The trek that day was very hot. As they moved away from the Guiding Bear, with the large mountains always within sight, but getting farther away, Mother Sky breathed more and more scorching breath on them and Sister Sun shone more and more brightly. They found that their steps slowed and they did not seem to go as far that day.

Enga felt that her questions did not get far either. She asked many of her tribe the same questions. Did you sleep well last dark time? Did you hear anyone moving around? Did you get up and move around? Did you see Tikihoo get up? Most of the answers were the same. Yes to the first one and no to the others.

She did begin to suspect several people, though. Some had added their own opinions when she questioned them. Most of them had opinions about who killed Panan One Eye.

Vala and Hama told her they thought that Tikihoo had killed Panan. Even Hapa said he now thought this. Vala reminded her how Tikihoo had shunned his body when it was recovered. Enga had thought a lot about that, and had decided that it was probably a tribal thing for Tikihoo. She had heard of other peoples who did nothing with their dead. They thought bad things would happen if they went near them, or touched them. Maybe even if they looked upon them. But maybe Vala was right. Bodd Blow Striker at first stated that he thought the killer was Mootak Big Heart, but then changed his mind and thought it was Tikihoo who had killed Panan. He gazed into the eyes of Vala while he gave his changed opinion. She returned his intent look with a half smile.

Hama and Hapa would not say why they now thought Tikihoo had killed Panan. That made the mind of Enga confused. Could it be that Hapa had killed Panan? He had been on the other side of the river for a long time when he went to bring Mootak back. Was he the one Mootak saw? He could be asking for help from Enga in order to find someone else to accuse.

Enga had still not found out what bothered Hapa, the thing he did not want someone to know. In this time of confusion, Enga probed the mind of Hapa to see why he thought Tikihoo had killed Panan. She had more success this time in his mind. She found some thoughts of Tikihoo, but they were not thoughts that she had killed Panan. They were very different thoughts.

Ongu Small One and her mate, Sannum Straight Hair, both cast suspicion on Hama herself. It was true that Panan had opposed her in many of her decisions. Enga was not sure that would compel Hama to kill him. Enga always remembered, though, that the birth-mother of Hama had not been a good tribe member. Hama did not act like her mother had, but they were of the same line. She began to realize that, in the fog, anyone could have waded across the river to do it.

Cabat the Thick, along with the new male, Fall Cape Maker, made it plain that they thought the obvious killer of Panan had been Mootak Big Heart. He had not kept it private how much he wanted to have the storytelling job of Panan very soon, and Panan was not giving the job over to him. Mootak had also been on the other shore with Panan when no one else had been there that they knew of. Fall did approach Enga later and tell her he was not certain that Mootak was the slayer, but that it seemed he had to be. Also, he did not want to contradict Cabat, who was trying to convince others.

If Mootak did see someone, someone he thought was a spirit, Enga knew that it could have been a person. Hama or Hapa? Who could have sneaked away and crossed the river to kill him?

As to who killed Tikihoo, most thought that it was the same person who killed Panan.

That made sense to Enga. A sudden thought came to her near the end of the walking time. If Tikihoo had known who killed Panan, whom she had cared for, maybe she had been trying to tell Fall and Jeek who that was. Maybe that was *why* she was killed. But that did not tell Enga *who* killed her.

Chapter 28

Enga Dancing Flower was very glad when the trekking for the day ended. Her strength was returning, but she still felt more weak than had been normal for her before she had lost the baby seed.

As dark time approached and the breath of Mother Sky cooled, Ung Strong Arm and Lakala Rippling Water came to sit with her as they gnawed at the tough jerky. As terrible as it was, and as much as everyone disliked it, there was some alarm that it would run out soon.

It will be a good time and I will be happy when I can get back to hunting, Ung thought-spoke. *I do not feel like I am doing what I am meant to do when I do not hunt.*

I am the same with my singing, Lakala answered. *I am supposed to sing for the tribe at every dark time. When I am not singing...the tribe needs to sing. And to dance.* She looked at Enga.

Enga agreed. Who would disagree? No one on the trek was being the tribe member they were supposed to be. *When we are settled in the new place, this will be far behind us. Our trek will be told as Saga. We will be like we once were. As soon as we reach our new home.*

If they found a sizeable herd of mammoth and could do a kill soon after that, that would be excellent and they would be fed and content. After a time, they would need more than one good kill before Cold Season so they could make jerky to feed the tribe through the time of much dark and of short light times. Enga hoped Dakadaga would take care of them when they got to the new land. She clamped down on the thought that it did not feel like Dakadaga was caring about them on this trek.

They finished eating and Ung and Lakala moved away a short distance to lay out their sleeping skins. Hama had not called for a council or Saga or music and dancing. Tog Flint Shaper, who had eaten with Fall Cape Maker, Bodd Blow Striker, and Vala Golden Hair, came to sleep beside Enga. As she lay, falling asleep with the arm of Tog draped around her, she realized she had more tribe members to question. She had not asked her questions of the younger ones, Jeek, Gunda, Teek Bearclaw, Akkal Firetender, Mootak Big Heart, and the other young ones. She would start with Mootak when she awoke.

However, while it was still deep dark time, she was awakened by a rustling noise nearby. She opened her eyes and saw Mootak, lit by Brother Moon, crawling from his sleeping skin near his parents, and walking to the edge of the group.

Was he walking while still asleep? She had known some to do that. Sannum Straight Hair and Cabat the Thick both used to when they were younger, and Mootak was the child of Sannum.

If Mootak went outside the circle of sleepers, there would be danger to him. They had not seen a cat of sharp tooth for many moons, but the large animal with the heavy shell and the deadly tail roamed these parts, as well as wolves, bears, and other cats. A mouse scurried away as she raised herself onto an elbow. She had not secured her pouch well enough and the mouse ran away with a piece of her precious jerky. At least he had not taken all of it. She cinched her pouch tightly and stood to hang it on a nearby pine branch.

When she looked around, Mootak was out of sight. She must find him so he would not come to harm. She crept to the place she had last seen him and looked around. He was standing not far away, beside a white-barked tree and his shoulders were shaking.

As she approached him, she could hear his soft sobs. She did not want to startle him, so she shuffled her feet in the undergrowth. He looked up and she saw, by the light of Brother Moon, tears glistening on his cheeks.

Mootak Big Heart, are you troubled? she thought-spoke to him, being sure to shield her conversation from the rest, some of whom might not be sleeping.

He nodded, his long, straight hair swinging forward. It was the hair of Sannum Straight Hair. He looked more and more like him as he got older. Sannum had been most kind to Enga and Ung when they were small and were first brought into the tribe. Enga would always love him, and so felt much warm feeling toward Mootak also. It made her ache inside that he was in such distress. He had been that way ever since the death of Panan, she knew.

I would like to ease your pain. She ran her hand across his head and onto his shoulder. He still shook with sobs, silent now. She squeezed his shoulder to convey her goodwill. To her surprise, Mootak threw his arms around her and they stood, hugging, for a time.

Eventually, Enga thought-spoke again. *Would it help you if you talked to me about your troubles? I would like to hear, again, what you saw the night Panan One Eye was killed.*

He nodded against her breast, then straightened. *Mother Sky had sent a breath of fog that I could not see through well. What I saw was not clear. But I did see a very white Spirit and I did see Panan One Eye. I saw her lift the heavy rock.*

Enga received the picture from Mootak as he sent his thoughts to her. She saw the white shape and she saw Panan. The white shape bent to pick up a large rock. The shape had long hair, hanging down, not braided. She wished the fog would part so she could see more clearly, but the mist was thick. She thought the Spirit looked white only because of the fog.

Could the Spirit be a person? she asked.

A dead person? One who walks after death?

No, I mean a person who is alive. I mean a member of the Hamapa tribe. Not a Spirit, but a person who looks like a Spirit in the misty breath, the thick air that Mother Sky sent to us.

Mootak frowned and considered this.

Enga continued. *Could a Spirit lift a heavy rock? A person could.*

He nodded.

Did you see that the Spirit was a female and not a male?

His eyes grew big and round. *I did say it was female, but I do not know that. I am not sure.*

And how did you know the rock was heavy?

It was hard to lift. It was large. And it crushed Panan One Eye when she…or he…

Mootak started gulping back sobs and could not finish his thought-speak. But Enga saw the rest through the vision he sent.

She now knew that someone with long hair had killed Panan. That might help her in her questioning. She held Mootak until he calmed, then led him back to his sleeping skin. His parents had not awakened. Neither had Tog. She slipped beside Tog and, in his sleep, he put his arm across her body again.

Chapter 29

Enga Dancing Flower hung back to approach Jeek as they walked. He had seen her doing private thought-speak with the others during the last sun time and at this one. He felt left out, as he had helped her the last time someone had met a violent death in the tribe. Now she was dropping back to walk beside him. Maybe she would want his help now. He hoped so.

Are you trying to find out who killed Tikihoo? he asked as soon as she was walking next to him.

She smiled at him. He grinned back as she answered. *I am. I am also trying to find out who killed Panan One Eye.*

Do you want me to help you?

She looked surprised at that.

I did help you find the killer when we were living in our village. I could help now.

She looked at him and thought private thoughts, then thought-spoke to him. *Yes, you did help. Maybe you can now, also.*

The grin of Jeek grew wider. *What do you want me to do?*

I am asking questions about the dark time when Tikihoo was killed. You can help me do that. Here are the questions I ask. Did you sleep well in the dark time when Tikihoo died? Did you hear anyone moving around? Did you get up and move around? Did you see Tikihoo get up?

Jeek was puzzled and frowned. *Why do you ask about the death of Tikihoo? I would ask questions about the death of Panan One Eye.*

Hama has told me to ask questions about the death of Tikihoo. You will find that some of them will tell you what they think about the slaying of Panan One Eye after they answer these questions. I am more and more certain that the same person killed both. But now I will ask you to answer these questions.

Jeek thought for a few moments. *I did not see or hear anything at the time Tikihoo died. I believe everyone slept well that night, as we were all tired from walking and we were hungry, eating nothing but the terrible Hooden meat.*

They walked a few steps without communicating before Jeek continued. *You want to know who I think killed Panan One Eye. Why do you think it was not Mootak Big Heart? He was the only one with Panan One Eye. Everyone else was on the opposite side of the flooding water.*

The flooding was going down during the night, Enga answered. *Someone could have waded across and done it. I believe Mootak Big Heart when he says he saw someone lift a rock and smash the head of Panan One Eye, then roll him into the water.*

It was not a Spirit? He says it was.

Jeek, do you think a Spirit would do that? I will tell you something no one else knows. You must not reveal this, but it will help you when you ask questions. Her thought-speak became cloaked even tighter in a darker shade of blue, the color of Mother Sky just before she stormed. *The Spirit, or person, had long, straight hair.*

Jeek stopped walking to absorb this, then started up again after the person behind him bumped into his back. His thoughts whirled. That would mean that there were only some members of the tribe who could have killed Panan. The hair of Hama was dark and curly. That of her birth-daughter, Gunda, was wavy and as red as Sister Sun when she met Brother Earth at the end of sun time. Enga herself braided her hair. Her birth-sister, Ung Strong Arm, had wavy hair that did not grow very long. His own birth-mother cut hers short. Ongu Small One wound her braid around her head. Who were the females with long, straight hair? Lakala Rippling Water, Vala Golden Hair, Fee Long Thrower, and...who else?

Of the males, Sannum Straight Hair and most of the other males had long, straight hair. Tog Flint Shaper wore his in a topknot and Bahg Swiftfeet wore two braids. Even Hapa and Akkal and Teek had long hair. Only Cabat had shorter, curly hair.

Another thought came to him. What if someone who wore braided hair had unbraided it, as they sometimes did, and let it hang loose? That happened for sleeping sometimes, as well as at other times. Maybe Ung and Zhoo, his birth-mother, were the only two females and Cabat the only male who could not be the killer because of the length of their hair.

Could Mootak Big Heart tell that the hair was straight? Could not wavy hair look straight in the fog that lay on everything at that time? he asked Enga.

She did not know the answer to that. *I did see the happening through the mind of Mootak Big Heart, but I cannot answer that question. The vision was unclear. Maybe you are right. The hair could be wavy.*

I will ask the questions and tell you the answers when we stop to eat and sleep.

Enga told him who she had questioned and they divided up the rest.

After she left him, he wondered if he should have told her about the gestures that Tikihoo made to him and to Fall Cape Maker shortly before she died. He would tell her later.

Jeek had not looked forward to making camp with this much eagerness since they had started the trek. He was energized by helping Enga.

* * *

Enga Dancing Flower was pleased that young Jeek wanted to help. He was clever and could converse more easily than she could with the younger tribe members, the ones nearer his age. Meanwhile, she would talk to some more brothers and sisters as they trudged onward.

She had not yet asked Tog Flint Shaper, her own mate, what he thought about her questions. Nor her birth-sister, Ung Strong Arm and the mate of Ung, Lakala Rippling Water. She would also question the mother of Jeek, Zhoo of Still Waters, since Jeek would not be a good one to do that. This last thought made her wonder if she should be the one to talk to those closest to her. Maybe she would talk to them, then Jeek could also do it. Maybe she would ask about Tikihoo and he could ask questions directly about the death of Panan One Eye, so they would not be saying the same things.

Satisfied with that plan, she looked around for Tog. She found him. He was carrying Sooka, but the mother of the baby girl was not near them. Vala Golden Hair hung on the arm of Bodd Blow Striker, opening her mouth to softly laugh at something he had thought-spoken to her. He had been falling under her spell of flattery for some time now.

Putting Vala out of her mind, she caught up to Tog and started making nonsense noises to Sooka to make her laugh before she sent Tog her private questions.

I have been asking many of our tribe these things. I should ask you also.

He willingly answered that he neither saw nor heard anything. *But, Enga Dancing Flower, you should not be doing this. If someone traveling with us killed both of them, that person will not want you finding out who he is.*

Or who she is. She took Sooka in her arms. It was wonderful to hold the baby. Sooka giggled when she made a funny face. Enga put her nose to the top of the head of Sooka and breathed in the pure scent of the baby. Enga wondered if she would always miss the baby she never had.

Do you think a female or a male killed them? Tog asked.

I am not certain. It could be either one.

Yes, Hamapa females are strong. Our males are strong, too, even the old ones. You are correct. It could be either. Do you have any ideas about this?

She shook her head and the ends of her braids ticked the baby. Sooka laughed, showing her one glistening tooth in her bottom gum. A Hamapa baby would have all of her teeth at this age, more than six moons.

That was all she could find out from Tog. He had no ideas on who the killer of Tikihoo was. She saw Bodd stride away from Vala and start walking next to Fall. She handed the baby back to Tog, with great reluctance—Sooka smelled so sweet and felt so soft. She had to talk to those two, though.

Not wanting Tog to know she was questioning Fall and Bodd, she made the excuse that she had to step aside and relieve herself. When Tog was a good distance away, she returned and sought out the Gata males. She was glad they were behind Tog.

Bodd had nothing at all to add. Fall told her about the hand motions she had seen Tikihoo making to him and Jeek, wondering if they had had anything to do with what happened to her.

She was worried. Scared of something, or someone, Fall thought-spoke. *She made motions like this.*

Enga watched very closely as he tried to repeat them. He screwed up his face like he was crying and balled his fists, turned them in front of at his eyes, then pointed. *She pointed to the riverbank.* Then he put his hands on his hair and brought them down several times.

Crying? Enga asked. *And indicating someone with long hair?* The long hair agreed with what Mootak saw.

Maybe. Fall then mimicked cradling a baby, and walking slowly.

Enga puzzled over these actions. She had come upon Tikihoo crying on the day Enga named the Hooden female. The hair of Tikihoo was short and curly. Did she merely wish that she had long hair? Was she crying because she did not? But Mootak said the slayer had long hair. Did Tikihoo mean the same thing?

Enga shook her head. Those thoughts did not seem right.

Fall could not add any more, so Enga went to seek Zhoo of Still Waters, the Healer.

Chapter 30

Enga found Zhoo of Still Waters near the rear of the group. Zhoo had stopped for a moment to give herbs to Ongu Small One for a belly ache. When Enga asked her the questions, she did not know anything about the matter of Tikihoo. Zhoo did not even know the things that Mootak had told Enga. She said she had been busy caring for those with feet that hurt and those who did not feel they could eat any more of the bad-tasting jerky. Zhoo had been dealing with many things. Enga asked if she could give Zhoo any help. However, Teek Bearclaw, the older son, was assisting her, Zhoo said.

Will Teek Bearclaw be the Healer some day? Enga asked.

Yes. We are planning for that. He learns very quickly and is a great help to me.

Enga was glad to learn that it was going well for Zhoo and for Teek. She wondered what the future held for Jeek, the younger son. She had always had a special affection for Jeek. It occurred to her that, when they stopped for the night and she and Jeek exchanged what they had learned, she should relate the actions Fall showed her.

She next sought out Ung Strong Arm and Lakala Rippling Water who, as usual, were traveling side by side. They had both slept with a deep sleep the night Tikihoo died. Enga decided to ask them about the time Panan One Eye was killed also, but they had not seen anyone leave the group, except the ones who had gone to the water to help those across who had been left behind. It was a confusing time, they said, because the tribe was moving to and fro and the fog was so thick it was hard to tell who was who.

Enga was dissatisfied with all the questioning, except the information from Fall. That might mean something, if someone knew what it was. Maybe Jeek would be able to make sense of that. He had been standing near when Tikihoo had given the gestures to Fall.

* * *

Jeek was excited to talk to Enga Dancing Flower when they stopped that night, but he could not do it right away. Bahg Swiftfeet had run up one of the rocky outcrops and thought he had seen a herd of mammoth far, far away. If only his seed giver, Mahk Long Eye were still alive, Mahk might have been able to tell what animals Bahg had seen.

Did you see trunks? Hapa asked Bahg.

Were there tusks? Cabat the Thick thought-spoke.

I have told you, Bahg repeated, *I saw a large herd and think they might be mammoth, but I could not see well enough to know that they are mammoth for certain.*

The whole tribe thrummed with excitement and hope as they lay down their loads and got ready for the night.

How many days of walking will it take to get to where they are? Hama asked.

Bahg shook his head. *They are very far away. By the time we get to where I saw them, they will move.*

That is true. Hama pondered to herself a moment. *At new sun, on our next time of walking, let us run up to the tops of the high rocky hills and look often.*

Jeek looked around them. There were long stretches of flat land, but there were also hills. Some were high and would take many hand lengths of Sister Sun to climb. But some were not so high. Most of the slopes were covered with the spiny plants that pricked his skin. This land was so very different from the village they had left behind. It was as if Sister Sun were a different Sun, also. And Mother Sky had never worn such a deep blue-colored hue as she had here.

As Sister Sun lowered herself, she sent out spectacular rays of golds and reds. Jeek knew this was pretty, but if they were still there at new sun, those colored cloud garments could gather and bring trouble for the Hamapa.

Akkal Firetender had been gathering long grasses on the walk that day. They were dry and brown in this hot place where Sister Sun had more strength than where they used to live. Akkal scraped out a small pit in the dirt, piled the grasses into it, and lit it with a spark from the fire he bore.

The Hamapa did not have a Saga that evening, but they danced to the singing of Lakala Rippling Water into the dark time to celebrate seeing a herd. Brother Moon shed a bright light from the half of his face that was showing and the many eyes of Dakadaga shone steady in the hot air.

Jeek did not want to interrupt the dancing of Enga. She was having a good time, he could clearly see. But when she left the circle of people cavorting around the small fire to get a sip of water, he ran to her.

When can we talk about what was found today? He almost jumped up and down in his excitement.

You have found out something? You know who killed them?

He did not want to disappoint her, but he could not mislead her, either. He shook his head. *No, no one knows anything more than we already do. But there is something I did not tell you earlier.*

She drew him away from the others, into the darkness outside the circle of light cast by the flames.

Even in the dark, Jeek could see her smiling at him, encouraging him to tell her his thoughts.

I did not tell you about Tikihoo. She came to me and to Fall Cape Maker, together, and she was trying to tell us something.

Enga nodded at him.

Did Fall tell you this?

He did. He said she made motions with her hands. But he did not know what they meant. Tell me what you saw and maybe we can figure this out. You and I together, Jeek, are clever, are we not?

Now it was the time for Jeek to give a huge smile. *We are clever. Maybe we can tell what she was trying to say. I will do what Tikihoo did.*

That is a good idea. I will try to understand what you are telling me.

Jeek thought that would probably not happen, since he did not know what the motions meant. But he started waving his hands. *She motioned toward the water. No, wait. First she acted like she was crying.*

Enga nodded, encouraging him to continue.

Next, she…I know what she was doing. She was telling me that the killer of Panan One Eye has long hair.

Yes, that is what I thought when Fall Cape Maker did that motion, running his hands down from his head. What did she do next?

Next she acted like she was holding a small child.

Enga raised her eyebrows. *What could she be trying to tell you with that?*

Jeek did not know. *You can not figure it out, either?*

Enga started to leave, then turned back and replied. *This will take a lot of thought. There are many things that Tikihoo could have been trying to say. Maybe she wanted long hair. Maybe she was afraid of a person with long hair. I do think she was afraid of someone. If we can figure out who that is, we would know what Tikihoo tried to tell you.*

If we knew what she tried to say, we might know who killed her.

That is true, Jeek. We must think about this. I might have an idea, but I am not sure that I do. I can not tell you now since I am not certain.

He felt his shoulders and his spirits sag. He would have to wait for her to tell him. There was nothing else he could do.

Chapter 31

"Some paleontologists find it ironic that for tens of millions of years both camelids and equids evolved in North America, only to migrate into and survive in Eurasia and South America, while they vanished in near time in their evolutionary heartland (Hulbert 2001)."

—*Twilight of the Mammoths*
by Paul S. Martin, p. 39

Enga Dancing Flower was shaken out of her deep slumber by Tog.

Awake! We must try to get to a place that is higher. It was not quite time for Sister Sun to appear, but there was no sign that she ever would. Mother Sky was dark. Her eyes were all closed, or hidden behind cloud clothing.

Tog pointed to the very dark cloud garments in the distance, where Sister Sun should be rising. Long streaks of gray ran from them to the flat ground. Lightning flashed between them and the ground. Rain was coming.

Hama says we must not get caught in a flood again. Tog stood over her, slinging his pouch over his shoulder and tugging at their sleeping skin so he could fold it.

Enga jumped up and shoved her belongings into her pouch, then took an edge of the large pack and helped pull. The tribe headed for a high hill that looked close.

They walked for a long time, though, before they reached the foot of the hill. It was nearly as high as the mountains that had made them turn and alter their direction many suns ago. The dark clouds were moving closer and rumbling came from them.

Tog Flint Shaper, can we get our burdens up there? She pointed to the top.

Maybe Hama heard that thought, because she sent out an urgent scarlet public message. *We do not need to get to the top. We only need to get higher than this low ground. We must all go with as much speed as we can.*

With a bit of grumbling and a lot of grunting, everyone helped, and little by little the burdens were dragged and carried upward. They encountered plants with sharp spikes that they soon learned to avoid, when they could. Many of them soon bore torn skin from the pricks.

When they wanted to stop, Hama and Hapa urged them on, higher and higher.

When they were halfway to the top, Hama let them rest.

Rest, however, did not last long. The storm was upon them. The bright, flashing spears that Mother Sky threw sparked almost without a moment between them. Her rumblings crashed above them. Enga felt they were going through her. Mother Sky wept more tears than anyone had ever seen. The rain tears pulled some of the plants with sharp spikes out of Brother Earth. The plants came crashing down, rolling past them, some of the plants catching the flesh of the Hamapa.

It went on and on. Mother Sky snarled and growled with so much raucous, hostile noise that Enga thought She might fall from her heights and lie flat on top of Brother Earth, leaving no room for the Hamapa. Enga found it hard to breathe.

Enga could not see through the torrent for more than the length of her arm. She heard a cry that she thought came from Akkal Firetender. She tried to move toward the sound, but was blocked by a river of mud washing down the slope. What if Mootak Big Heart had attacked Akkal? She shook her head. No, Mootak was not a killer. She had told herself this many times. But what if the actual killer had struck Akkal?

The sound of the rushing water became less. The lightning spears and grumbling crashes moved away at last. Soon Enga could see her tribe. They were all there, huddled on the side of the steep hill, all alive, all drenched.

But Akkal crouched over his pouch and his tip of horn where he carried the fire, and he wept. *The fire is gone! I have lost our fire!*

Hama went to him quickly, sloshing through the mud and hopping over the piled up thorn plants.

New fire can be gotten. It can be created or found. She stroked his back and laid her head on the top of his bowed one.

He stopped sobbing after a time.

Hapa leaped off the ground and waved his arms. *There is fire! It is coming this way!*

The spears from Mother Sky had lit some of the plants afire, even through the solid wall of rain. The wildfire raged above them, coming down from the top of the mountain with a roar.

The first thought of Enga was that Akkal could gather this fire. But she realized in the space of another thought that they were in danger from it.

Now the tribe scrambled to gather their things and rush down from that place. Running and sliding, they reached the bottom of the slope in a much shorter time than they had climbed up. When they got to level ground they kept running, glancing behind at the fierce, licking tongues, devouring alike the uprooted plants and the ones still standing. At least the lower ground was not flooded. The water had all run off to somewhere else.

When they had outrun the slowing flames, they dropped their belongings, but Hapa, Akkal, and a few others ran back toward the fire, burning itself out on the soggy flat ground, to claim a bit of it for the tribe.

When they returned, the face of Akkal shone with happiness as Sister Sun broke free of the clouds. Akkal bore smoldering embers he had just collected in the tip of his hollow mammoth tusk. When his moss that was still wet had dried out, he would cover the embers with that. For now, slightly damp dried grasses filled the horn. As always, a thin plume of smoke followed Akkal.

Mootak walked beside him and they grinned at each other. Cabat the Thick, who was the seed giver of Akkal, waddled up to them and pulled Akkal away from Mootak, being careful of the horn he carried.

The shoulders of Mootak sagged and his smile vanished. Enga went to Mootak and gave him a hug. She was ashamed and angry that Cabat made it so obvious he thought Mootak was a killer. He had not thought so at first. What had made Cabat change his mind? He had first argued that the killer was not Mootak. She overheard some thoughts from the others that agreed with Cabat. Some had the opinion that Mootak was the killer, but if he were banished, there would be no Saga, so that they had to act as if he were not a killer. Enga could not tell exactly where these partially veiled thoughts came from, but they came from more than one of her brothers and sisters.

The tribe did not go much farther and stopped well before dark time fell upon them. At the request of Hama, Bahg Swiftfeet and Tog climbed part of the way up a small mountain as the others were settling down. They came running back to report that a mammoth herd was not far ahead of them.

Some Hamapa wanted to continue right then, but Hama and Hapa both convinced them to rest.

What to do about the herd was discussed at length.

If we do make a kill, Ung Strong Arm pointed out, *we will have no way to bear the meat with us.* The meat from a mammoth would usually last the tribe many, many days, and many more days for the portion they dried. Now, they had no firepit for drying. Since they were moving, they could not drag that much fresh, undried meat with them.

Fee Long Thrower had a good idea. *Bahg Swiftfeet tells me that the herd also contains at least two camels. They are smaller and maybe we could get a camel instead.*

The camels were easier to kill. The Hamapa preferred the meat of the mammoth, but they had often eaten camel meat in the past. Also, the hide of the camel was softer, although smaller.

It was agreed by everyone that they should try to get a camel for now.

At first sun it may be that we can send out a hunting party, Hama thought-spoke to them, standing on a flat rock near the pine woods they had come upon at the base of the mountain. A stream gurgled from within the forest, not far away from the sounds of it.

It was a happy group who made camp. Enga, Ung, and Lakala gathered as many gourds as they could carry and went into the forest to bring water back.

Enga thought she had never seen such a pretty stream. It rushed over rounded rocks and swirled in eddies at the foot of a small waterfall created by the rocks. As they approached, a small frog leaped into the water, leaving widening circles behind. A turtle, sitting where it caught a ray of sun on a rock near the far bank, slowly turned its head toward them before abruptly splashing into the water also. If only they could live here, she thought.

The three females dipped the gourds, collecting the fresh water. Ung and Lakala rose and started back. Enga stretched her legs in front of her and stayed another few moments, listening to the sounds of the water and of a slight breeze rattling the needles of the trees. From deep into the woods a bird gave an alarm call, warning the woods of the intruders. The water at the last few places had not tasted good. In some of the places, the water sat without movement and had a scum on top. Enga cupped her hand for an extra taste of this fresh, delicious water.

Enga strolled back to her tribe with a feeling of peace that she had not had for some time.

As soon as she reached the group, that mood vanished.

Cabat held the upper arm of Mootak, shaking him, and sending out ugly thoughts.

Chapter 32

"One member of the genes (*Camelops*) was Yesterday's camel (*Camelops hesternus*), also called the western camel… Abundant and widespread…[i]t probably both browsed and grazed on a diet of leaves, small plants, fruit, and grass. It was larger than living dromedary camels. The legs of Yesterday's camel were about 20 percent longer than those of the modern dromedary, but otherwise the two probably looked alike."

—*Ice Age Mammals of North America*
by Ian. M. Lange, p. 158–159

Enga Dancing Flower set down her water gourds with care, then rushed to Cabat the Thick. She grabbed his arms from behind, pulling him from Mootak Big Heart.

When others saw what was going on, they clustered around. There was much racket in the head of Enga from her tribe.

What is Cabat the Thick doing?

What are you doing, Enga Dancing Flower?

Cabat the Thick, why are you shaking our Storyteller?

Enga sent a thought to Cabat herself. *Cabat the Thick, do not try to harm Mootak Big Heart. Do you want to lose our Story? We will have no past, no history, if you harm him.*

Cabat shrugged himself out of her grip and spun to face her. *Do we want a killer for a Storyteller? Do we want a killer in our tribe?*

Enga felt a fire build inside her, but before it could erupt, Hama stepped between them, pushing them apart with her hands. Hama looked at Cabat and sent him a message Enga could not read, but it was not a friendly thought. Cabat glared back at Hama, returning thoughts to her.

Hama turned away and lifted her arms to address the tribe. *No one will harm a Hamapa brother or sister. This is not done in our tribe. We are not like the Mikino and other tribes. We are Hamapa, The Most High People.* She turned her head to throw a glance to Cabat, then continued. *If a brother or sister wants to charge another with a misdeed, then that must be done in peace. We will not harm one another.*

After one last hostile scowl at Cabat, Hama stalked off, leaving Cabat and Mootak, and Enga, as everyone else melted back from them. After a few moments, Cabat shuffled away.

Enga saw the tears Mootak had managed not to spill trembling at the edges of his eyes. She put her arm around his shoulders and drew him away so the tears could run down his cheeks where the others could not see.

* * *

Jeek was so excited he could barely keep his feet still. He wanted to dance and to leap. He, Jeek, was going to go along on the camel hunt! A real hunt, as a spear thrower. He had been wanting to do this for many summers.

He strode beside pretty Gunda with music in his head, and joy vibrating inside his body. He carried the spear that Ongu Small One had given him, the one he had carried on the last unsuccessful attempt. Fee Long Thrower had told Jeek that he should go on this hunt. Fee and Ung usually led the hunts and were leading this one.

Now, here he was, heading toward the herd that had again been sighted at first sun. It appeared the mammoth and the two camels had moved closer to them and were but one or two hand lengths of Sister Sun through Mother Sky away.

The group of female spear bearers and the males, one of whom carried the large mammoth skin, made barely any noise as they walked through the long grasses.

Ung Strong Arm and Fee Long Thrower, as the two best spear throwers, were in the lead. Behind them, Enga Dancing Flower, Ongu Small One, and Hama carried spears. Then came Jeek and

Gunda. Tog Flint Shaper and Bahg Swiftfeet brought up the rear, carrying the skin in which they would drag the carcass back.

The party halted when Ung shot out a thought: *Halt! We are near.* They all crouched in the tall grass, waiting for the next signal. The spear throwers arranged themselves in a row so they could all throw without hitting each other. Tog and Bahg stayed behind them.

Jeek could smell the herd. He heard them ripping grasses from the ground as they grazed. The ground shook when the feet of a huge mammoth pounded down. The animal was trotting. Was it running toward them or away from them?

He saw the short wavy hair on the head of Ung inch upward, over the grass, until she could see what was happening. He tensed, feeling Gunda do the same beside him.

A new thought-speak came from Ung. *Both camels are very close, one a bit more so. When I give the signal, each person with a spear will throw at the one nearest us. The mammoth herd should then run away, and the other camel will go with them. We must hit the camel or it will run away.* Another few moments passed, then the signal came. *Throw! Now!*

Jeek leapt up. The camel was even more close than he had thought it would be, barely four lengths of a Hamapa male away from him. He drew his arm back and flung his spear. The other spears flew through the air, like a flock of birds.

As the first stone tip hit the hide on the flank of the camel, he jerked his head up. Then the other spears found their mark, two in his neck and two in his body. The camel keeled over while the rest of the animals thundered away, flattening the grass and raising plumes of dust.

Jeek was the first to reach the animal. It jerked a few times while he stood well back watching, then lay still. When he saw that his spear was one of the two in the neck, he grinned. The one Gunda had thrown was the first, the one that hit the flank. He glanced at her to see if she was disappointed at her aim. But Gunda looked pleased also. It was not important which spear dealt the death blow. It was important that there would be food for everyone. Fresh meat. And not Hooden meat, either. The Hamapa had eaten camel many times before and valued the hides. It had been a long time, though, since they had eaten camel and Jeek was not sure he remembered what it tasted like. He did not remember that he disliked it, which made him happy.

It was a perfect night. Akkal Firetender cleared a dirt area and made a fire in the middle of the space out of grasses and dry fallen wood they had all helped gather from the woods.

The camel meat was carved into small chunks by the males with their obsidian knives, then sticks were set up to roast it over the fire. While it cooked, Lakala sang thanks to Leela, the Spirit of the Hunt.

Jeek wished they were in their new land and could have a proper evening, the kind they used to have before this journey. At least there was a song. When Mootak Big Heart stood and started to thought-speak, Jeek realized there would be a Saga also.

In the faraway times, the mammoth traveled with themselves. Herds of mammoth only. At times, the cat of long tooth would snatch one of the babies. At other times, a jaguar, the cat of the flat head, would drag away one of the older members of the herd. At still other times, a dire wolf, the huge long-legged wolf, would run at them and pick off the most slow runner.

Mammoth are smart creatures. They knew they needed some protection. They needed a way to make this not happen so often.

Once, when a herd was watering as dark time approached, two camels came to water at the same time. They were unafraid of the large mammoth. Many other animals kept away from them in fear of their size. But not the camels.

The leader of the mammoth herd conferred with the two camels. A bargain was made. If the camels would travel with the herd, the mammoth would pull down tall branches for them to graze upon.

The camels agreed to travel with the mammoth herd. Most of the time, this was a benefit for the camels. But the mammoth were more clever than the camels. When the herd was threatened, the largest of them formed a circle around the babies and the pregnant females. They left the camels outside the circle. The camels were much more easy prey, since they did not have long, sharp tusks, and could not crush animals with the weight of their huge, flat-bottomed feet.

To this day, camels travel with herds of mammoth. Whenever we desire camel meat and camel skin, we can get them.

Mootak left out the fact that none of them, camels nor mammoth, were easy to get. Camels were more easy, but not easy. Jeek knew that this was not part of the Saga, which was one he had heard before, but he could not help thinking the thought. He had heard tales of difficult camel hunts. This one had not been difficult, though, and he was so proud that his spear had helped bring down the animal whose meat was giving off such a succulent aroma, roasting above the fire. The males had carved it into small chunks so that it would cook quickly. He did not let others know of the pride he was feeling, since it was not the Hamapa way to be proud of yourself instead of the whole tribe.

There was a short dance, but no flute and no drum, just the singing of Lakala. Then Sannum Straight Hair, who stood tending the roast, sent out a bright scarlet message to let everyone know that the meat was ready.

Moisture leaked from the corner of the mouth of Jeek as he stood, waiting his turn. When he finally got a big hunk, speared on a stick because it was too hot yet to touch, he made himself wait until it was cooler so he would not burn his mouth. But the waiting was very hard.

Chapter 33

"Nine different kinds of owls, including three extinct species, are found at Rancho la Brea... The Great Horned Owl, *Bubo virginianus*, was also very common."

—*Rancho La Brea: Treasures of the Tar Pits*
edited by John M. Harris, p. 35

After walking all of sun time once more, Enga Dancing Flower was feeling discouraged when they stopped. She knew there would be no fresh camel meat. What had not been eaten had been gone at first sun. The tribe had been careless with the meat. They had not guarded it, since no one could have stayed awake. One of the young boys of Ongu Small One and Sannum Straight Hair had climbed a tree and tied it to a high branch. That had not worked to protect the delicious meat from the hooting birds of the night. Enga had heard them in the distance, and when the tribe awoke all realized the birds had probably taken the meat. If not the dark time birds, then something that could climb well had taken it, for it was gone.

Once more, they gnawed on the jerky. Enga could barely swallow it, remembering how Tikihoo relished the meat that had been a gift from her people. She knew she must eat it, though, or she would not have strength to walk again the next day. With only a part of her mind, she continued to probe for a stray dark thought from someone who had slain two people. She found some dark thoughts, but they were about hunger and fear, never about the killings.

Tog Flint Shaper, eating next to her, sent a thought to Hama. *How much longer will we walk? When will we reach our new land?*

Enga wondered why he asked such a question. How could Hama answer that? She did, though.

There is a large flat-topped hill ahead of us. You and two others will climb it at first sun. Choose two to go with you. This may take you all of sun time. You will see if there are mammoth herds. If you do not see them, look for a watering place. We will all wait until you return. If you see either a herd or a watering place that is of a good size, we will go there. It could be that our new home will be near.

Their old village had been half a sun away from a watering hole, close enough to go to it to hunt mammoth, but far enough not to make the animals stay away from the water. Even though her body did not feel that it had taken in enough meat, she fell asleep content, knowing that the end of the trek may be near. She was also content because Tog curled up next to her and stayed there for all of dark time.

Before Sister Sun fully appeared above Brother Earth, Tog and the two others set out. The group that remained was camped almost in the shadow of the large mountain with the flat top, since the shadow cast by the early Sister Sun stretched long across the ground and across the water. Hama and Hapa decided to stay where they were until the scouting party returned, rather than move toward the mountain. The place where they were had a small spring of good-tasting water and a group of needle-leafed trees for shade from the blistering rays of Sister Sun.

Teek Bearclaw and Bahg Swiftfeet went with Tog. Enga watched them climb the rocky slope until she could see them no more. They must have found a route to the top on the other side of the mountain because they headed around the rock, out of sight.

She sent a thought to Tog, a small one saying she hoped their mission brought success. But no reply came.

A strong thought, filled with pain, drifted through her mind. She knew it came from Hapa. He was the one who had thoughts that were different. This one was more open than any she had ever gotten from him. It was a picture of Tikihoo. It was not of Tikihoo killing Panan, it was of Tikihoo caressing Hapa. They were in a dark place, alone, in the vision.

Had Hapa and Tikihoo mated together? Had he wanted to? That would be something he would not want Hama to know. Enga decided to leave this secret with Hapa, since Tikihoo was gone and nothing good would happen if anyone knew of this deep, secret thinking.

The Hamapa huddled in the shade of the fragrant pine trees as Sister Sun journeyed. Enga felt the sticky tears of the needles drip on her, but she didn't pay much attention. She looked up through the trees at Mother Sky. She had changed color on the journey. Now She was the blue of deep, deep water. When Enga stared at Her, She seemed to have depths Enga had never noticed before.

Sister Sun was also different in this place. She gave off more heat, and She seemed more large, and her light more bright. Everything was different here. Were they under a different Mother Sky and a different Sister Sun? On a different Brother Earth? He had changed the most.

Enga missed the old village so much that a pain arose inside her ribs. When she closed her eyes with the pain, tears ran down her hot cheeks. How were they to live in this place? Were there any other people like themselves here? They had seen none. They liked to trade with others, to get things that they did not make themselves.

Tog had always traded his flint spearheads and cutting tools. The Hamapa had also traded obsidian knives. But was flint to be found here? Was obsidian here?

What would become of the Hamapa, Enga wondered. Other tribes, starving, had died out. That was why the Hamapa had set out on the trek. She knew they had to go. Still, she wished they could have stayed in the old home.

Some of the Hamapa strolled around examining the plants that grew here. Enga noticed that Zhoo of Still Waters stayed with Fall Cape Maker much of the time. Since she was the Healer, she needed to look for plants she could use. She also needed distraction, since her birth-son Teek was away on the mission.

Enga sent thought-speak to Fee Long Thrower and also to Zhoo, asking if they had heard anything from Teek and Bahg. Neither of them had. With the scouting party out of sight, Enga worried that something bad might have happened to them.

At last the scorching breath of Mother Sky grew a bit more cool and Sister Sun sank to embrace her lover, Brother Earth. Enga lay on the ground, watching the eyes of Mother Sky begin to appear and to twinkle. Brother Moon peeked up, then rose to be among them.

Enga took a bit of comfort from Brother Moon looking exactly the same as he had at the old village. At least something was unchanged.

Just before she fell asleep, a message floated into her head from Tog. *We are weary. We tried very hard to make it to the top of this place during sun time, but are not there yet. The way there is steep and rocks slide beneath us, making it hard to make progress. We will reach the top before high sun, we are certain of that. So far we have not been able to see any herds or any large watering places.*

Enga was sure Tog could feel her smile as she returned her own thoughts. *Be safe and step with care. I know that two of you could carry one injured one down, but do not make that necessary, if that is in your power. I will miss you this dark time, but I will imagine that you are curled up next to me.*

Fee and Zhoo both received reassurances, too, and broadcast them to the tribe. Enga slept well knowing that the three males were alive and well.

As others were awakening, Enga heard the squalling of Sooka, the baby girl of Vala Golden Hair. She saw Fee Long Thrower rise and stoop to pick up her own infant, Whim, then approach Vala to help with Sooka. Poor Fee, thought Enga. Then she joined them and took Sooka herself.

The child was not like a Hamapa child, but she was bright and eager when she was not crying. It seemed to Enga that Sooka got bored and liked to be entertained, since she could not walk yet, nor even crawl. Enga ended up playing with both babies. She hid her face with her hands, then opened them with her eyes and mouth wide. Both babies squealed in delight every time she did it.

Eventually, Whim toddled off to follow Ung Strong Arm and Lakala Rippling Water into the woods to gather wood for the fire.

Sooka, who could now sit on her own, followed him with her eyes.

Yes, you can do that, too, she thought-spoke to Sooka. *You can get up on your legs and walk. Watch how Whim does it.*

The little girl tilted her head and looked at Enga. When Enga smiled at her, she grinned back, showing her smooth gums with the one bright tooth, growing more long every day.

See? This is how you can crawl. Enga picked her up and set her on her tummy. Sooka pushed up with her chubby hands, trying to get her tummy off the ground. Enga encouraged her, wondering if Vala was doing anything for the development of her child.

Well before high sun, Teek Bearclaw sent an excited broadcast to the whole tribe. *We are at the top. We can see a large herd at a watering place that might be only a few more suns from here. And we can also see a second mammoth herd in the distance. They are here!*

Even with the three missing brothers, the tribe celebrated with song and dance at dark time, as well as they could without them.

Jumbled, joyful thoughts flew back and forth.

This is our new land.
We can settle near here.
At last we have arrived.
Soon there will be fresh meat.
New mammoth skins.

The thoughts flew on and on about building a new village, new abodes, finding a place to keep the fire safe, and a place to have First Couplings and births and first Red Flows for the young females. The Sacred Cave on the Holy Hill had been used for those purposes at the old village. Enga wondered if any place could ever be as ideal as that had been.

In spite of the optimism and hope, she wept silent tears for her old home, and for the baby she had lost on this awful trek. She also wept for the two lives lost, Panan One Eye and Tikihoo.

Sooka, who was in her arms, touched the cheek of Enga and wiped a tear with her stubby finger.

Sooka, you make me feel better. She almost told her she wished that Sooka were her birth-child, but before she sent that thought-speak, she realized that would not be a good thing to tell the child.

At first sun, Ung Strong Arm came to Enga Dancing Flower. *Why were you sad? Why were you not rejoicing with all of us?*

Enga realized she had not kept her weeping as private as she had wanted to. *Just missing the old place,* she answered, not wanting to tell Ung everything she had mourned for at dark time when it was such a happy time for Ung and all of the others.

Chapter 34

The scouting party returned by high sun the next day. They came down the mountain more quickly than they went up.

We used the same path when we returned. It was more easy coming down than the climb up was, Tog told her.

Hama decided they would walk for the rest of the day, even though a good part of it was already gone. It seemed to Enga that they went with more speed than usual. There was a bounce in her step, and in that of all the others. The burdens they carried and dragged seemed lighter, and the sweltering heat, while still very hot, was not complained about. There were towering rocks that shed intermittent shade. They did tend to linger a bit in that coolness, but still covered a great deal of distance.

They trekked through three more suns before they reached the large body of water. They got there early, soon after Sister Sun appeared. The lake had been created by a massive pile of dead trees, which blocked the flow of a creek. Rivulets trickled through the branches and a small stream ran out.

Hama got their attention. *We will trek part of one more day, upstream, and look for a good spot.*

Enga Dancing Flower turned to Tog Flint Shaper. *Do you think she means a good spot to stay? A spot where we can live?*

I am sure of it. We are nearly at our new land.

Enga noticed the others having excited small conversations, too. They were all thinking alike, that they were almost home. The tears that now ran down the cheeks of Enga were not for sadness. She saw the cheeks of others shining and wet in the sunshine, also.

The water gourds were quickly dipped in the lake and filled, then they hiked to the other end of the lake, where a large stream entered it. That took more time than Enga thought it would, but they kept up a good speed, and soon, in about three hand lengths of

Sister Sun through Mother Sky, came to a place that almost looked familiar, though it was in this strange land.

Needled trees grew along the banks of the stream, leaving a small area clear where they stopped. The trees stretched in every direction and were dense. There would be plenty of wood. Less than one sun away across the water was a strange mountain. It was as if the Spirit who created Brother Earth had put one small flat-topped mountain on top of a much larger one. Enga hoped the mountain held a cave that could become sacred to the Hamapa.

For the rest of the day, until darkness started to creep across Mother Sky, the tribe worked on setting their things in various places, picturing how they would construct the new village, where the firepit should be, and the wipitis. Hapa thought they would need to find a place that was not so crowded with so many trees, but others thought they could live among them.

Some of the females ventured into the forest, carrying spears. When they returned with three fat rabbits, Enga clapped her palms together in glee. Ung Strong Arm, who had killed one of the animals, told them there was a place along the stream, not far away, where the land was more clear of trees. It did not take the tribe long to move their things to that place. It looked like there had once been a fire there, probably from one of the burning spears that Mother Sky sometimes threw during a storm. Some of the tree trunks were charred, but it had been some time ago because the ground was now covered with soft grasses and small bright flowers.

Hama stood in the middle of the clearing, turning around and nodding her head. *Yes, this is the location of our new village*, she thought-spoke to everyone. *At new sun more exploration will be done.*

Soon, we must send some males, announced Hapa, *to see if the nearby mountain contains a place for a Holy Cave.*

Hama nodded at this, too.

As they, once again, distributed their scant possessions around the clearing, imagining what the finished village would look like, sounds of something approaching came from the forest—steps on crunching branches, muffled by layers of fallen needles.

Enga did not think they were the footfalls of animals.

Someone approaches on the deer path we discovered in the woods, Ung thought-spoke to her.

The tribe turned to face whoever, or whatever, was visiting them.

They emerged from the trees one at a time, having walked the path single file. The first one was a male. He was a Tall One like Stitcher had been, tall and narrow, but with skin the color of acorns. He wore his straight hair in a topknot, secured with a bone, just like Tog Flint Shaper did.

Two more stepped into the clearing. They were all males and all wore short skirts that had been stitched together.

Yes, Enga thought to herself, *these are Tall Ones, people like Stitcher, and like the tribe we encountered that told us the mammoth were not far.*

These did not wear the hides of horses like that tribe, though. The fur on the stitched footwear looked like that of bison. Maybe the clothing was bison hide also.

The one who had appeared first ran his gaze over all of them, then settled on Hapa and nodded to him. Hapa turned to Hama, who nodded back at the strangers.

Enga remembered that these people were led by males, rather than by females, abnormal though that seemed.

The males made noises that Enga now knew were the way they communicated, like the Hooden did. But no Hamapa could understand the peculiar speech. They listened to the sounds in silence, trying to read the thoughts of the newcomers. If only Tikihoo were still with them.

Sooka picked that time to start babbling. Enga was holding her. Vala Golden Hair had handed the baby to Enga while she sorted through her things.

One of the males smiled at Sooka and made sounds back at her. She reached for him and all three of the males grinned. He stepped forward and let Sooka grab his long, thin finger.

Another of them motioned, first to the Hamapas and then pointed across the stream. All three of the visitors nodded and all three gestured to the tribe and then across the water.

Enga wondered if they wanted the Hamapas to go over there, but that did not seem like what they were trying to tell them. Maybe they lived there.

The leader reached into a pack he wore on his back and drew out some strands of tiny, tinkling shells, strung on sinew. He handed them to Hapa, who gave them to Hama. The males exchanged puzzled looks, then comprehension came to their faces, that Hama was the leader, and they all nodded their heads to her. They then stepped back into the woods and vanished into the trees.

As everyone crowded around to see the gift that had been given to Hama, relief flowed through the group. They had neighbors and the neighbors, though not like them, were friendly.

Darkness now fell and Akkal lamented that he had not started a central fire. Hama assured him that they would pick a place for it at new sun, but for this dark time, they would bed down as they had on the trek, on their skins in the open. The weather was not yet cool and they had time to construct wapitis to dwell in before Cold Season.

Enga, who still held Sooka, saw that Vala was kneeling on her sleeping skin. Enga walked toward Vala to return the baby. Vala jerked when she saw Enga coming and put her hand into her pouch.

Later, as Enga was falling asleep with Tog at her side, she wondered what Vala had not wanted her to see.

Chapter 35

A grunting noise awakened Jeek. He rose on his elbows, realizing that all of his tribal brothers and sisters had slept past new sun. That was a rare thing for them to do. This was a sign of how relaxed they felt here.

He gazed upward, into a color that must have been created when Wawala, the Spirit of the Waters, mated with Mother Sky. She looked deep and liquid this day.

The grunting continued, even grew louder. He peered with sleepy eyes past his recumbent tribe to see several strangers standing at the edge of the clearing, next to the trees. They were people like the Hamapa, but dressed differently. At first he thought they had shiny legs and feet, but then saw that they were merely wet. These people must have come from the other side of the water and waded across the stream where it was narrow.

There were two females and two males. The males both scowled, but the faces of the females seemed friendly. The two females also looked very much alike.

Jeek jumped up and smiled at them. He also quickly sent a thought-message to the tribe. *There are strangers here. Wake up, everyone.*

Hama was the first to spring to her feet. She approached the two females solemnly and nodded at them. They both nodded back.

Hama tried to ask them which person was the leader. *I am Hama. We are the Hamapa, the Most High People. We have come from far away. Who is your leader?*

The two females glanced at each other. For a moment, Jeek thought they had not understood the thought-speak of Hama. Then one of them answered in brilliant colors so that everyone could understand. *We are the Yamapa, the Most Good People. We dwell across this water. We live in the Most Good Place.* The other female gestured to the creek as the first one thought-spoke. *You are welcome to dwell here, on this side of the water.*

The other one asked, *Do you have enough to eat?*

For now, we do have enough to eat. We will hunt soon and store food for Cold Season.

Hapa, who stood nearby, spoke up. *Does this place have a Cold Season?*

The taller male told him that it would come at the end of the Hot Season, after a cooling time.

Jeek thought this place must be similar to their old home, just much warmer.

One Yamapa female, the one who had spoken first, told them she was called Yama, The Most Good Female. The other said she was Yama Doe, The Second Most Good Female.

It was puzzling that there seemed to be two leaders. They looked alike and would be impossible for him to tell apart. He thought they must be twins, people who were born at the same time from the same birth-mother.

They started to turn, to leave, when Sooka started babbling. She was in the arms of Enga, as she had been a lot lately. The four Yamapas stared at Sooka, their mouths dropping open.

Yama Doe thought-spoke first. *Our tribe has a baby such as this. Where did she come from?*

Vala Golden Hair spoke up. *She is my baby. Her name is Sooka. Her seed came from a Tall One.*

Yama and Yama Doe both nodded. *Yes. That is true for our baby also. Her seed giver is a Tall One.* After a brief silence, Yama thought-spoke one more time. *The Yamapa would like to meet together to feast and dance when you are ready.*

Hama smiled at this and agreed to let them know when that time came. *How far away do you dwell?*

Yama waved her sturdy arm in the direction of the strange mountain. *In the shadow of the hill, at Tiki Vis. It is a journey that takes less than half of one sun.*

At that, they hurried into the trees and left.

* * *

Enga Dancing Flower held Sooka out before her and dangled her, pretending to dance with the baby, sending her a thought-message that the new home of the Hamapa was a good place. There were neighbors who were friendly, and there would even be a large gathering soon. Sooka smiled back, showing her nearly toothless gums. Enga bestowed a kiss on top of her sweet-smelling head, then set her down to sit and watch while the tribe went about continuing to decide what would go where in their new village.

Hama and Hapa, with Cabat the Thick helping because he was one of the older members of the tribe, walked the perimeter of the clearing, gesturing and conversing with each other. Enga was relieved those three were getting along.

Akkal Firetender picked a spot in the middle of the clearing far away from overhanging branches, and with a nod from Hama, began trying to dig a firepit. The ground, however, was hard and unyielding. Tog Flint Shaper came to him with a wide, flat blade. Together they found a stout branch, notched it, and fastened the flat stone to it with sinew. After Tog broke the ground with his chopping rock, Akkal and Tog were able to dig the dirt and scrape out a pit with the blade on the handle.

Meanwhile, Hama and Hapa had set out pine branches to mark where they thought the dwellings would go. They ranged them in a semicircle around the firepit, just as they had been in the old village, with the wipiti of Hama and Hapa sitting a bit removed from the others. It would be larger to accommodate meetings, and because the greater wipiti told everyone who the leader was.

All the wipitis would back up to the swift stream. Enga sat for a short time in the location where her wipiti would be, listening to the voice of the water. She thought she heard the whisperings of Wawala, telling her all would be well. Sooka stopped her constant fidgeting and listened to the water also. Enga knew she would enjoy falling asleep to the sound of the water running over the rocks that were scattered in it. Maybe they could rearrange the rocks to make an easy way to cross the water here, instead of walking to the other end of the lake to cross where a narrow dribble emerged from the dead trees that had become piled there.

Another large wipiti would be put at the other end of the semicircle for the unmated males. Vala Golden Hair chose a place for her wipiti nearest the spot for that of the unmated males. Enga thought that Vala would probably be inviting them all to her place. She wished Vala would settle on a mate so that jealousy would not arise and so that there would be no bad feelings among the males. Bodd Blow Striker walked to Vala and squatted beside her. Maybe he would be her mate. That would be a good thing, Enga thought.

There were not as many unmated males as there had been at one time. There were Cabat and the two Gatas. Teek Bearclaw and Mootak Big Heart would probably move in there also. Those younger males had been living with their parents. The son of Cabat, Akkal Firetender, would also live with the unmated males.

Her thought returned to Vala. The birth-mother of Vala had been the Hama after Aja Hama had died, but Enga had never liked her. The present Hama was the birth-sister of Vala, so also the daughter of that Hama, but the two females were not alike in any way. Vala was like her mother. Roh Lion Hunter, who was now Hama, was more like her seed giver, Kokat No Ear, a person Enga had liked very much.

Enga finished unpacking her belongings in the space she and Tog had picked out. Now they would need many mammoth tusks to build the dwellings. They would spread mammoth skins over the tusks, after they were set into the hard ground. The skins would be their walls, weighted with rocks, maybe brought from the water, or maybe from the rocky hills around them. It would be many suns, maybe many moon cycles, before everyone had a wipiti, so Hama announced that they would try to get two, or maybe three built before Cold Season. Maybe all the females could stay together and all of the males. They would complete their village after Cold Season was over.

A ripple of dissatisfaction came from Vala. Bodd had left her to finish setting up by herself. Enga concentrated on the emanations, poorly cloaked, and understood that Vala did not want to live with other females during the dark time. She much preferred to be with the males. It made Enga sad that Vala seemed to prefer the males over her own baby, too.

Sooka brought Enga out of her musings. She squalled and let Enga know that it was time for her to eat.

Chapter 36

Jeek was happy that his mother, Zhoo of Still Waters, the Healer, was spreading her things next to the place Enga Dancing Flower was using. He liked being near her. He would also like to be near Gunda, but she would live in the large tent with her parents, Hama and Hapa.

Vala Golden Hair had finished nursing Sooka and had handed her back to Enga. Now Vala struggled to straighten out her sleeping skin on the ground. It would not lie smooth. Jeek saw the problem. There was a root where she was putting the mammoth skin. He thought there had been a large tree growing nearby at one time.

He passed Enga and Sooka, who were watching Tog Flint Shaper drive wooden stakes at the edges of their future wipiti, and walked over to Vala. He watched for a moment before pointing out the reason for the bump. *Do you want me to try to chop this root so the ground will be flat for your sleeping?*

She looked annoyed. *I can move over. There is no need to do that right now. Maybe at a later time.* She snatched up her pouch that lay near where Jeek stood. What looked like a stone wrist or arm band dropped out of it. She grabbed it and stuck it back into the pouch in a hurry. The stone was shiny and polished.

That is a pretty stone, he thought-spoke to her. It reminded him of something, but he did not know what. *May I see it?*

It is nothing. She turned her back to him and he left, a bit angry because Vala was so rude to him. *No wonder most brothers and sisters do not like her*, he thought to himself, keeping this soft and private.

The tribe had bustled about, arranging things, hauling stones from the river that they might want to use, gathering twigs and logs from the woods, and this was after they had walked for so many suns at a fast pace. However, no one was tired. They were energized by finally reaching their goal.

We have arrived! Hama thought-shouted, in the most brilliant hues she could summon, as Sister Sun began to disappear. *There will be a celebration now that it is dark time.*

They rushed through eating the meager fare. The dried jerky was almost gone and very little remained of the three rabbits from the day before.

Akkal Firetender gobbled his meal and finished before anyone else. He piled the dried twigs he had gathered into his pit and fanned the flames until they blazed upward as if they wanted to greet Mother Sky. He piled on log after log. Jeek knew he would not always be so wasteful, but it was a night to celebrate.

The tribe gathered in a half-circle around the fire. He saw that Sannum Straight Hair had already found a small hollow log so he could beat the rhythm, and Fall Cape Maker held the flute of Panan One Eye. He smiled inside at the thought of dancing. Gunda took her place near her parents, Hama and Hapa, with her two younger sisters. When she looked his way, he felt his skin glow.

Hama stood before them, her straight back to the fire, her dark curls glistening in the light of the flames. She raised her arms high and spoke. Jeek leaned forward to catch every word of the Pronouncement.

"Hoody! Yaya, Hama vav."

Listen! Yes, the Most High Female speaks.

"Hamamapapa ah yaya wipiti mana."

The Hamapa have a good place to stay.

"Ta Ka. Ta Wawala. Ta Dakadaga."

We give thanks to the Spirit of the Earth. We thank the Spirit of the Waters. We thank the Most High Spirit.

Jeek saw that his eyes were not the only ones that held tears and his cheeks were not the only ones that shone with wetness in the firelight. A slight wind led the flames into a slow dance for their joy.

There were no thoughts that were not thankful and cheerful as Hama nodded and Sannum started the slow beat. There were songs giving thanks to almost every spirit, the voice of Lakala Rippling Water and the notes from the flute of Fall Cape Maker blending, rising and falling. Jeek danced next to Gunda and he thought his insides were growing too big for his skin, he was so full of happiness.

* * *

After the most festive time the tribe had celebrated since they left the old village, Enga Dancing Flower collapsed on her sleeping skin while Tog Flint Shaper went to the edge of the woods to eliminate before he slept. She had danced her best, giving all that she had to thank the Spirits for the journey and for this place. She felt she was strong and well, in her body, from the ordeal of losing the baby.

She gazed at the stars above, each one clear and bright, some winking to show that Mother Sky was kind to the Hamapa at this time. She glanced toward the place where Vala Golden Hair lay with Sooka at her side, sound asleep. Enga felt she needed to keep track of Sooka and always make sure she was well taken care of. She knew other Hamapa felt like that, too. No one trusted Vala to care for her own baby in the proper way.

After such a glad celebration, a dark thought came to Enga. This thought was never far away for her. In this tribe, there was a person who had killed, twice. The deaths of Panan One Eye and of Tikihoo had not been accidental. Someone had drowned Panan and someone had pushed Tikihoo from the cliff. The only sign of what had happened were the hand movements Tikihoo had given to Jeek and Fall Cape Maker. Enga thought about these. She recalled the motions. There were motions of crying, then pointing to the riverbank. Then an action that was like combing long hair. The last motions were of rocking a baby and walking slowly. Again, as every time she thought of these things, she wondered if she would ever figure them out.

Enga missed Tikihoo for what she could have told them, and for her ability to speak with others, but she also missed her quiet presence. If only there could be a way to tell her Hooden tribe what had happened to her. They must wonder. Someone there must be missing her, Enga thought.

An idea came to her. She could ask each Hamapa separately, in private. She could show the motions to each person. If one of them had killed Panan, would that person recognize what the motions meant? Would the thoughts of that person give away the Hamapa who had killed Panan, then Tikihoo? Enga was convinced that Tikihoo was pushed from the cliff because she knew who killed Panan.

She clamped her thoughts shut when she saw Bodd Blow Striker pacing in a ring around the sleepers.

Chapter 37

"The Abric Romaní [Capellades, Barcelona] provides 10,000 new fossil remains about the domestic activity of Neanderthals. The diversity of the stone raw materials used for the lithic industry and also the variety of the animals hunted show long-term occupation of this specie in this territory. The distribution of the hearths and the archaeological remains from level Q reinforce the division of the occupation surfaces into sleeping, animal processing, tool knapping and rubbish areas."

—from IPHES (The Catalan Institute of Human Paleoecology and Social Evolution) news https://iphesnews.wordpress.com/2015/08/26/ recovered-a-container-excavated-on-a-neanderthal-occupation-floor-from-60-000-years-ago/

At first sun, Fee Long Thrower and Ung Strong Arm started to discuss a hunt. The tribe needed mammoth tusks and new hides soon, before the breath of Mother Sky turned cold. They talked of having the hunt at the next new sun and then began to plan the details. Enga Dancing Flower listened to them and the other females gathered by the smoldering firepit for a time, then went to check on Sooka.

She found the baby sitting upright, all alone, on the sleeping skin of Vala Golden Hair. Vala had left the baby alone. Sooka was starting to whimper, but was not crying yet. Enga scooped her up and rocked her. The child smiled up at Enga and Enga had to smile back, although she felt much anger toward Vala.

When Vala came sauntering back, Enga asked her why she had left the baby alone.

I had to go to the woods.

Enga assumed she had been to the place, off the deer path, that had been chosen. It was far enough away that the odor of their waste would not be too strong, but close enough to get to when they needed it. But Vala had been gone a long time. Too long to go that short distance, Enga thought.

Enga answered Vala. *Then why did you not take Sooka with you? She does not like to be by herself.*

She gets into too many things.

Enga grew more angry. *Sooka cannot even crawl yet. How could she get into things?*

Vala looked away, a faint frown creasing her forehead between her brows.

Sooka started kicking and whining. Enga thought she must sense the tension between the two females. *I will tend her then, since she is too troublesome for you.*

Enga walked away with the baby, feeling the sharp spikes of anger that Vala directed at her back. While Vala was in such a bad mood, Enga did not want to leave the child with her, even if she was her birth-mother.

However, it was not long before Vala approached Enga, who was playing finger games with Sooka and tossing pine cones at the edge of the clearing. Sooka had such long fingers for a baby, Enga thought she would be another one who could stitch.

Do you know where Tog Flint Shaper is? Vala asked.

He is scouting the rocks for material to make spear points with.

That same line deepened between the brows of Vala. *Do you know where Bodd Bow Striker is? Or Fall Cape Maker?*

I do not. They may be looking for spear shafts. There is talk of a hunt soon.

Yes, I know. I hope we get a large animal so there will be much hide. Vala glanced down at her mammoth skin garment, thin and worn, as were all of the garments of the Hamapa.

Enga wondered if Vala thought she would get the first skin for her own use. That would probably not happen. She realized she had not cloaked that thought thoroughly when Vala narrowed her eyes.

Vala looked at the ground for a moment, then looked up and gave Enga a wide smile that felt cold. *Enga Dancing Flower, do you think you could find someone to watch Sooka while I show you something?*

I can take her with us.

Do you think that would be good?

How far away do you want to go? Enga asked.

Vala looked at the flat-topped mountain across the water. *To that place. Will you go with me? I think I see a cave we could use, but want to make sure.*

Enga thought that would be a good thing to look for. Hapa had wanted to send some males to do that, but she thought it had not happened yet. *Yes, I will go with you, and we can take Sooka. We will take turns carrying her.*

Vala pressed her lips together, then smiled again. *That will be fine. Let us go now. You can carry her first.*

They walked around the end of the lake and made it to the foot of the mountain soon. Enga had thought it would take much more time to get there. It was nice that the mountain was so close, especially if there was a cave there that the Hamapa could use. They needed a sheltered place for Akkal to keep the permanent fire, and a place for the rites of first Red Flow for females, for First Coupling for new mates, and a place to give birth. It looked very much like a break in the rocks above them could be an ideal cave.

Enga and Vala started climbing up the slope, which was not too steep at first. The slope grew more steep, however, and soon they wanted a place to rest. A ledge was ahead and Enga was glad when they made it there. The ledge was narrow, but flat. She had carried Sooka by herself on the climb so far. It would be time for Vala to carry her next.

From the ledge, it appeared that the cave was not far above them. They could not tell how deep it would be inside, so they decided to go all the way up to it after a short rest.

Look how far we can see. Vala sat beside Enga and they both dangled their legs over the edge. Vala gestured to the plain below. *There is the river, the lake, and we can even see our settlement.*

Yes, our brothers and sisters look small from here. Enga had set Sooka on the back of the rock, but the baby lay down and rolled over toward the edge. Going over the drop-off would not be good. Sooka would probably not survive the fall. Enga had not known that Sooka could roll over so well. That was a good sign of progress. Maybe the child would walk some day.

If you stand up, you can probably see more, Vala thought-spoke.

Why did not Vala stand up and see for herself? *Why do you want me to stand up? Why do you not do it?*

I am very tired from the climb.

Enga felt a tension coming from Vala. She stood, holding Sooka, but could not see much more than she could seated. She turned around to tell Vala that and found Vala standing next to her, very close behind her. Vala had a smile on her face that seemed genuine this time.

Enga Dancing Flower! Vala Golden Hair! What are you doing here? Tog Flint Shaper, with Teek Bearclaw and Bahg Swiftfeet, came scrambling down the slope from behind a thick stand of pine scrub. Enga had been concentrating so hard on what Vala was secretly thinking that she had not sensed their presence. Vala had not sensed it either, Enga thought. Vala jerked her head toward them and stepped away from Enga and Sooka. Her smile was gone.

We are looking to see if that cave would be good for us to use. Enga pointed upwards at the opening in the rock.

Yes! It is a very good cave, answered Tog. *We have just been there. It is dry and deep and does not shelter any large animals.*

Good. We can tell Akkal Firetender and he can bring some fire to it, thought-spoke Enga. She felt a wave of darkness coming from Vala. A coldness entered her and she wondered if Vala had meant to throw Sooka over the ledge. Or if she had meant to push both Enga and Sooka. Enga could not stop her arms from trembling as she held baby Sooka on the way down the mountain.

All of them returned to the place where their new village would be. Enga thought of it as their village even though nothing had been constructed but a firepit. She kept Sooka for the rest of the day, until dark time, when the tribe had another gathering. No new meat had been caught, so there was not much to eat. The mood was good, though, because they all felt ready for a hunt at new sun.

The Gata males had found straight, strong shafts for spears, and Tog and others tied some points onto them that he had already made. Tog had come back from the mountain with a few pieces of flint rock, but he had seen a place farther up that had much more flint for new spear points, and some obsidian lying as if it were a river coursing down the slope. Obsidian made excellent sharp-edged knives, so he would be back for that soon.

When Tog and the others had been on the mountain, they had moved around to the other side and had seen that a large herd of mammoth was close beyond it, and moving in their direction, toward the water. They could not see that the plains around the mountain had a place to trap the animals, so they would have to creep through the tall grasses and surprise the herd, trying to take out one or two that were the closest as they came to get water at first sun.

Enga loved the way the eyes of Ung Strong Arm glowed in the firelight with anticipation of the hunt. Akkal had kindled a blaze, not as large as the one at the last dark time, but of the usual size. If Enga faced the fire and closed her eyes, she could picture the half-circle of dwellings that would be behind her, the new mammoth tusks gleaming white in the fire, and the tanned hides stretched tight to keep out the breath of Mother Sky when it blew cold. On a warm night like this one, the door flaps would be thrown open, letting in the slight breeze and the leaping light.

Again, she danced almost until she could not move her limbs. Tog quit long before she did. The only dancers remaining as long as Enga were Vala, tossing her hair so that it shone like Sister Sun, and Bodd Blow Striker, who stayed close to Vala.

Chapter 38

"Columbian mammoths had very long tusks (modified incisor teeth), which were more curved than those of modern elephants. The largest known mammoth tusk, 4.9 metres (16 ft) long, belonged to a Columbian mammoth... The tusks of females were much smaller and thinner... At six months of age calves developed milk tusks a few centimetres long, which were replaced by permanent tusks a year later."

—from https://en.wikipedia.org/wiki/
Columbian_mammoth

Jeek had trouble falling asleep after the gathering. His birth-brother, Teek Bearclaw, would go with the adult males who would carry the largest of their skins, the skin that would be used for dragging the kill back to the tribe. The animal would be butchered and roasted, but most of the meat would be dried to eat during Cold Season. Fall Cape Maker had told them that he knew much about treating hides, so Hama had put him in charge of that.

Jeek himself would be behind the others, with the younger members of the tribe who were old enough to go along, the two little sisters of Gunda and the two little brothers of Mootak Big Heart. They would help however they could. Jeek ached to throw a spear with the females, but had not asked to do that for this hunt. Another time he would again, when the hunt was not so crucial.

Sooka let out a sharp cry, which was soon muffled, probably by the breast of Vala Golden Hair. She fed her baby, but did not do much else with her. Enga Dancing Flower had held the baby, rocking her in her arms, for a long time after they came back from the mountain.

Jeek started to fall asleep with those hand signals from Tikihoo going around and around in his mind, as they had been doing for days and days. With a gasp, Jeek bolted upright. Now one of them became clear. Tikihoo had acted like she was crying, then right after that, had made the motion of rocking a baby. It all fit together. The baby had been Sooka and someone had picked her up and comforted her. Sooka had been on the riverbank.

He crept over to where Enga Dancing Flower slept to wake her and relate to her what he had figured out. Next to her, Tog Flint Shaper was sitting up late and talking with Bodd Blow Striker about the flint and obsidian they could gather. Tog waved Jeek away, giving him the picture of Enga sleeping and a stern warming that no one should wake her.

Jeek slumped back to his place beside his mother and his birth-brother, determined to talk to Enga at first sun. He knew how important it was that all the females be rested to throw spears long and straight and hard, so he was not too upset about Tog waving him away.

* * *

Hama sent out a wake-up message to everyone while Brother Moon still shone in the dark Mother Sky, surrounded by her many eyes.

Enga Dancing Flower sprang up, full of energy for the hunt. She grabbed the spear that had been prepared and ran to where Ung Strong Arm, Lakala Rippling Water, Fee Long Thrower, and the other spear throwers were tying wraps on their feet. She put hers on and walked with her spear to the edge of the clearing.

Hama and Hapa, with Cabat the Thick, stood in a row so the hunters could file past the Elders. Somehow, Cabat was now an Elder again. Hama had brought out her gourd and rattled it as the tribe chanted softly, giving a blessing to the spear throwers walking past.

After they got away from the village, they started running lightly. They had to go around the end of the dammed up water to get to the herd. In the dark they could not see if the herd was nearby or not. The still air did not send them any scent of mammoth or camel. Enga sent up a plea to Leela, the Spirit of the Hunt, *Let the herd be watering. Let us take an animal. Let us not starve.* Then she also sent the same pleas to Aja Hama.

The males and younger tribe members followed at a distance. On this hunt, they would stay behind until an animal was brought down. Maybe more than one would be taken if everything went well.

Enga felt the mind of young Jeek lightly touching hers, but she closed him off, needing to concentrate on the hunt.

When the females got to the end of the lake, they stopped to test the wind. It was slight now, but blew toward the hunters. Mother Sky often stopped sending her breath in the time just before Sister Sun appeared, and also in the time just after she went away. That was happening today. The air grew more calm as the sky started to lighten. The females nodded at each other. Their scent would not be blown to the animals if they were at the water. Enga had caught a faint whiff of mammoth before the air calmed, telling her that they were near.

The hunters moved away from the water and into the tall grass where they went slowly, creeping with the most silence they could manage. The grunts and lapping sounds of the herd came to them through the still air. The herd was taking water. That was very good.

Ung and Fee went before the rest. Enga saw the head of Ung poke up above the grass to see clearly where each animal was. She sent back the picture to all the females. On other hunts, at the old hunting grounds, the males would sometimes try to divide the herd, but that was not practical here with no place to hide, except in the tall grass, no woods they could spring from to surprise the animals.

The herd was relaxed, with the males and females intermingling and the babies in the middle as well as at the edges of the grouping.

Nearest to the hunters, two camels drank beside two large males. A female and a baby mammoth waited behind them.

They concentrated on the female and the baby. Ung and Fee drew closer and closer, Enga and Lakala behind them, staggered so they could all throw at once. The other females spread out to the sides to try to catch any animals that ran when the spears started flying.

Ung gave a silent signal, stood up with Fee and they both flung their spears. One hit the baby, the other hit the mother. Other spears followed, bringing both animals down. The baby fell onto its side and the mother to her knees.

A mighty blast came from the largest male mammoth and the group began to run, leaving the water. At first they headed toward the hunters who were flanking Ung and Fee. Vala and Ongu and Zhoo sprang up and ran away from the animals. The Hamapa males jumped up, ran toward the mammoth, and shouted, waving their arms. The herd kept coming toward them. The males turned and tried to run out of the way of the stampede. Enga was almost, but not quite, in their path. She had thrown her spear, so she yelled and jumped up and down.

When the herd was almost upon the fleeing females, Ongu, standing her ground, cast her spear, hitting a young male in the eye. As soon as the spear connected, the stampede veered and thundered away from the tribe. The male mammoth who had been stricken stopped, but stayed upright, swaying and shaking his head to try to dislodge the spear in his eye. The others who still had spears threw them at the animal. Then he was down. Enga sank to the ground in relief, as did a few others.

Now Fee Long Thrower called the males to come make sure all of the animals were dead. The males swarmed over them, stabbing with their knives and clubbing with rocks to finish taking the lives of all three. The baby was dead, but the other two needed to be attacked further.

With the rest of the herd well away and the dust settling, the animals were cut into smaller pieces that could be carried.

Enga had noticed, even in the flurry of the hunt, that these mammoth were large and healthy. They were the shorter-haired kind, the same kind they had encountered in their old home most often. She thought the long-haired shaggy ones must not like to live in this much warmer place.

The last one that had come down, the young male, had large tusks. The baby, another male, was not as young as Enga had thought, since he had tusks also, almost as long as those of his mother.

She marveled at the amount of hide and meat they would have. Akkal and the other males would be kept busy roasting and smoking meat for many suns. All would have to help stand guard over the smoking meat so that it did not get taken by animals. Juices sprang up in her mouth at the thought of the fresh roasted meat and smoked mammoth jerky. It had been a long, long time since she had tasted mammoth.

After the meat had been cut, Sister Sun was low in the sky. They must hurry to bring the catch back before the light disappeared. Enga wished they could go straight across the water. They were nearly opposite the place they needed to be and going through the stream would be a direct path and a lot closer. But they must go around the lake water.

Walking back, she had an idea. Much of the other bank of the stream was crowded with trees, but this side was mostly grassland. There were a few long-leafed trees next to the water, but only a few. She would tell Hama her idea and see if it was a good one.

The returning hunters were greeted with shouts and joy, even though the news had been relayed to Hama as soon as the animals were slain. Those who had stayed to guard the settlement thumped the females on the arms and back.

After the meat and hides were deposited, she sought out Hama and Hapa to give them her idea of moving the village to the other side of the stream.

It would have no protection, Hama thought-spoke among the three of them. *Would being closer to the herds and the cave be better than being here?*

It would not, Hapa answered. *If we lived on the other side of the stream, the animals would not come there to water if we were near it. They would be frightened of us. Maybe we should live nearer the mountain. That would also be on that side of the water.*

We should consider this, Hama agreed. She thanked Enga for the suggestion and continued discussing it with Hapa as Enga left them.

Jeek ran up to her. He had been trying to get through to her all day. She smiled at him and asked what was on his mind. He looked excited, but worried.

I have figured out what Tikihoo was trying to tell us!

You know what all the hand gestures meant?

Maybe not all of them, but some of them. The crying was that of a baby and the rocking was to say that a baby cried on the riverbank and was picked up and cradled.

Jeek, called Zhoo of Still Waters. *Come help with the meat.*

I need to go help Teek Bearclaw and the others finish cutting the meat, he told Enga, and ran off.

Enga sat against a white-barked tree to think about what he had said. The only baby who cried a lot was Sooka. Whim was much more calm and did not cry much. If he did start to cry, he would run to his mother. Sooka had been on the riverbank? How had she gotten there?

Enga Dancing Flower, will you help me?

Enga managed to keep her unfriendly thought to herself. *Not Vala Golden Hair again! I get so tired of helping her. She cannot do the most simple task by herself.* But Enga would rather help her than have Tog help her. She rose and saw Vala, beckoning from just into the woods. Bodd Blow Striker stood behind her.

Our feast will be even better with pine nuts. I love them and many others do also. Will you help me and Bodd Blow Striker gather them?

Enga suppressed a sigh, but gritted her teeth. *Why are you carrying that large knife?*

There may be a branch that we have to cut down. Bodd Blow Striker is so strong. He can cut thick branches for us if we need to do that.

Enga frowned. There were many, many pine cones on the ground. Why would they need to cut branches? She followed Vala and Bodd into the woods. Vala had something on her mind, but Enga did not think it was pine nuts.

Chapter 39

"It is intricately made with polished green stone and is thought to have adorned a very important woman... The bracelet was found inside the famous Denisova Cave, in the Altai Mountains, which is renowned for its palaeontological finds dating back to the Denisovans, who were known as homo altaiensis, an extinct species of humans genetically distinct from Neanderthals and modern humans."

—from "Stone bracelet is oldest ever found
in the world" by Anna Liesowska,
Siberian Times, May 7, 2015

Jeek watched Enga Dancing Flower follow Vala Golden Hair and Bodd Blow Striker into the woods. He caught some of their thought-speak. Enga asked who was keeping Sooka and Vala said that Fee Long Thrower was watching her so that they could be gone for a long time.

He also caught a current of unease from Enga. He kept looking until they were out of sight, frowning and thinking very hard. He tried to read any emotion coming from Vala, but could not. Bodd did not give off any thoughts either. He was focusing all his attention on Vala, as he usually did.

Vala had to have been close by when Panan One Eye died. She must have followed the others to the shore when they went to rescue those who were stranded. Tikihoo had told him and Fall Cape Maker that a person with long hair was there and that a crying baby was on the riverbank. Since no one else knew that Sooka had been there, Vala must have been the one who picked up the baby and soothed her. Tikihoo had feared the person. She had feared Vala.

Yes. It made sense now that he had fit it all together. Tikihoo knew that Vala had left her baby, had waded across, and had killed

Panan. That is why she feared Vala. Vala found out that Tikihoo knew of this, so it had to be Vala who pushed poor, scared Tikihoo off the cliff. And now Enga had gone into the woods with Vala.

Bodd was also there. Would he keep Vala from doing harm to Enga? Or would he do whatever she wanted him to? He had caught a gleam of something shiny in the hand of Vala. An obsidian knife?

He must get help.

* * *

Enga had followed Vala and Bodd deep into the woods. Now she stopped. *Vala Golden Hair, we have passed a lot of pine trees and pine cones. Why are we not picking up the cones?*

Also, Enga wondered how they were going to carry the tiny pine nuts. None of them had brought any pouches. Just the unneeded knife.

Vala had been walking ahead of Enga and Bodd behind Enga. Vala turned and faced Enga. There was no expression on her face. Her green eyes looked hard. When Enga tried to touch her thoughts she met a cold barrier. It surrounded Vala like a cape made of rock. Enga felt that she might not even be able to reach out and touch Vala through such a solid wall of thought. Vala tightened her fingers on the knife. The shiny blackness of the blade gleamed in the dark of the deep woods.

A flock of small birds took off from the tree nearest them. No birds sang. The forest was as quiet as death. Not the slightest breeze stirred the pine boughs or the leaves of the other trees.

Like a flash of blinding lightning in a storm, Enga saw the whole picture. She saw Vala, her pale body white in the mist, holding Panan One Eye under the water, picking up her crying baby, threatening Tikihoo, pushing her from the cliff. Too late, Enga realized she had not cloaked her thought.

The barrier of cold that had surrounded Vala broke away, and dark, hot, hostile waves of anger burst forth.

Bodd gripped the arms of Enga from behind.

In the next moment Vala leapt at Enga, the knife outstretched to cut her neck. The leap gave enough warning for Enga to raise her foot and kick the knife from the hand of Vala. The knife nicked Enga in the leg as it flew in an arc into the needles beside the deer path.

Enga had more strength than Vala did. She had always had that. That was a good thing now. With Bodd still holding her arms, she kicked at Vala and struck her midsection, knocking the breath from her.

Enga jerked her head back and cracked her skull into the nose of Bodd. He loosened his grip on her arms and fell to the ground, clutching his nose. Red flowed down his face.

Before Vala and Bodd got up, Enga sent a distress call to Tog and to Ung and to the whole tribe.

By the time Vala was trying to rise on one elbow, Enga heard many brothers and sisters crashing through the trees, snapping twigs and crushing leaves and pine cones. Large flocks of birds fled from other trees and they now all started to give out cries of alarm.

Tog reached his mate first. He glanced to make sure she was not harmed, then grabbed the hands of Vala. Vala had gotten up and shaped her fingers into hooks and her face into a picture of rage, ready to claw at Enga. Tog held her wrists behind her.

Others came running behind Tog. Hapa grabbed the arms of Bodd from behind, just as Bodd had done to Enga. The Red from the nose of Bodd streamed down his face and dripped to the ground.

Tog gave everyone a picture of what he had seen when he arrived, Enga being held by Bodd and Vala trying to attack her. He pointed out the obsidian blade, shining from the bed of pine needles, and Enga added a vision of Vala attacking her with it.

Hama broke through the crowd and stood in front of Vala and Bodd. Her sadness drew wetness from her eyes to run down her cheeks. Enga knew that her pain was because Vala was her own birth-sister. Enga felt her eyes sprout wetness also, thinking of how much she loved her birth-sister and of what great sorrow it would be if such a person as Vala had been the sister of Enga.

Anger and hatred continued to flow from Vala, almost turning the space around her red, the angry red of a flaring sunset or a devouring fire. Her breath came in short, noisy pants and she still struggled against Tog.

I did not kill Panan One Eye. The thoughts of Vala were strident. *Bodd Blow Striker killed him. Look into his mind—you will see that this is true.*

Bodd looked at Vala with his eyebrows up and his mouth open. *Vala Golden Hair, you are the one who killed Panan One Eye. You asked me to tend to Sooka after you took off your clothing, while you waded across the water. You said you would get rid of him so that we could be together.*

Bodd Blow Striker does not give the truth! That is not the truth!

Hama raised both arms. *Silence*, she commanded.

Hama led the way back through the trees with heavy steps, her head bent and her shoulders slumping low.

When they emerged from the woods, Enga wished that Hama had a wipiti she could go to, so she could close the flap and be alone. Hama must have caught that thought from Enga because she touched the shoulder of Enga with tenderness. Then she turned to face the tribe, and Vala.

Vala had continued to pull against Tog on the march, but now stood facing her leader and birth-sister with her head up and ice in her green eyes. They had never looked so much like the eyes of her mother. Bodd, with Red still flowing from his face, looked as defeated and discouraged as Hama did.

All the tribe stood around them. Sooka, in the arms of Fee Long Thrower was, for once, quiet and calm, sucking her chubby thumb.

The council was held immediately, while Sister Sun was still a little bit visible.

No one could tell what the truth was, but Enga thought that it was possible Bodd killed Panan when Vala told him to. That is what he eventually told them, although Vala was encouraging him to tell them that. Enga thought it might be true and it might not be true. After Fall Cape Maker told his Gata brother about the gestures of Tikihoo, and Bodd realized that Tikihoo knew what they had done, Vala had pushed her from the cliff.

It was decided that it did not matter which one killed which person. They both helped murder Panan in the beginning. Vala would be held responsible for Tikihoo and Bodd for Panan.

Hama looked like she would weep at any moment when she lifted her arms to proclaim that Vala Golden Hair was banished.

"Hoody! Yaya, Hama vav." Her voice broke, then she continued. "Vala Sha Doh Tikihoo tza. Poos Vala Sha Doh."

Listen! Yes, the Most High Female speaks. Vala Golden Hair slew Tikihoo. Vala Golden Hair is banished.

Hama then continued. "Bodd Cho Akk Panan Oh Zee tza. Poos Bodd Cho Akk."

Bodd Blow Striker slew Panan One Eye. Bodd Blow Striker is banished.

The voice of Hama quaked as she continued. "Dakadaga sheesh Hamamapapa."

Mother Spirit of the Sky, Dakadaga, bless the Hamapa.

Enga repeated the plea to Dakadaga in her own mind, adding a private one to Aja Hama.

Hama walked to Fee, who still held Sooka, took the baby and handed her to Enga. Now the tears of Enga flowed onto the baby, who looked up at Enga, her new mother, with wide, shining eyes and a gummy smile.

After the knife was returned to her, Vala walked away, heading upstream into the woods. Bodd followed with the same equipment. They were banished with only the clothing they wore and a knife for each one, as was the tradition. No one knew how long it would take, but they all knew they both would probably perish. Without a tribe, no one could stay alive.

Chapter 40

"Scientists...at the annual meeting of the American Assn. for the Advancement of Science said the most tantalizing signs of human presence are what appear to be human palm and finger prints on clay found in a 28,000-year-old layer of earth, and a number of hearths in various layers that go back perhaps 38,000 years... The prints, verified as human by police forensic scientists, were on clay that had been shaped to serve as a fire pit." [Found in Pendejo Cave in New Mexico.]

—from "New Clues Put Humans in New World 28,000 Years Ago" by Boyce Rensberger, *The Washington Post*, February 10, 1992

Hama told Enga Dancing Flower and Ung Strong Arm to go through the pouch that had belonged to Vala Golden Hair. Enga and Ung squatted with their shoulders touching, taking things from the pouch and laying them out to see if they could be of use to anyone else. When Enga found the stone bracelet, she had to stop what she was doing. She straightened her back and squeezed her eyes closed, picturing Tikihoo, her tall stature, her curly brown hair, this stone band always on her dark-skinned arm. When the vision of the broken body under the cliff came to her mind, she tried to think past it.

Enga opened her eyes to see Ung giving her a look of sympathy. Ung ran her hand up and down the arm of Enga to soothe her.

I will be back in a moment. Enga took the stone band and brought it to Hama. Enga knew she, herself, could never wear it. It was a beautiful thing, smooth and polished, fitting for the arm of a leader.

Hama understood at once. She took the band and put it onto her own forearm, nodding her thanks to Enga.

After Enga and Ung had gone through the things and laid them out so the tribe could choose what they wanted, Enga went back to where Tog Flint Shaper waited for her with Sooka. Enga was worried that Sooka, who had still been nursing with Vala, would not be able to have any milk. The baby had only one new tooth, although light marks on her lower gums told of more that would soon appear. The aroma of roasting meat permeated the village site. Enga would try to feed that to the baby.

Zhoo of Still Waters went through the things of Bodd Blow Striker. Fall Cape Maker, who had not communicated since his Gata brother was discovered trying to help Vala slay Enga, shook his head with sorrow when he was asked if he wanted to do look through the belongings of Bodd.

When the tribe ate at dark time, Enga chewed up the fresh roasted mammoth meat and gave that to Sooka. Sooka had no problem eating it and was eager to eat much more. It was a good thing that there was plenty of meat.

Even though everyone gorged on the meat, and even though two tribe members had been banished, the dancing that night was spirited and joyful. Fall eventually danced beside Zhoo, though without the energy of the others. Enga felt great relief that there was no longer a killer among them. Maybe the others did also.

Bahg Swiftfeet and Hapa had followed Vala and Bodd for a distance to make sure they kept going and did not come back. Everyone would be tuned for their thoughts for at least a moon and would know if they drew near again.

Enga was surprised how calm and happy Sooka seemed. She gave the baby a stick to chew on for the pain of teething. Maybe, Enga thought, the baby had been hungry, getting only milk. Maybe Vala did not have enough for the child, who was growing larger and larger. Enga was sure Sooka would be taller than Whim, the baby of Fee Long Thrower and Bahg, even though Whim was older by a few moons. Sooka was part Tall One and part Hamapa. Enga would always be aware of that. She came from people who spoke and did not read thoughts, but she also came from the Hamapa. Maybe she would learn to put hides together with the small, sharp bird bones that had been in the pouch of Vala. They had belonged to Stitcher. Enga had kept those for Sooka. She wanted her to have something of value from her birth-mother. And these were from her seed giver as well.

Enga would tell Sooka of the good in her birth-mother when she was older. About how Vala was the one who befriended Stitcher and was kind to him when no one else was. She would tell Sooka of the skill of her seed giver with the stitching implements, and how he had carved the Aja Hama figure. Maybe Sooka would be able to speak with the Tall Ones as well as thought-speak with the Hamapa.

After the dancing and singing, Enga and Tog lay next to each other, still in the open air, with Sooka between them. Construction on a new wipiti would begin at new sun, now that they had some tusks. Fall Cape Maker would treat the new hides and they would have protection when Cold Season came. The scent of the mammoth meat being smoked into jerky made this place feel like home to Enga.

Sooka made soft, wet sounds, sucking on her thumb, content.

Maybe they would move to the other side of the river. Maybe they would stay here. Maybe they would build a new village as good as or better than the one they had left.

These thoughts ran through the mind of Enga. She thought that Dakadaga approved of them when she saw the night eyes streaking across Mother Sky. She saw one, then another, then many others. Yes, Dakadaga was giving them a sign. She showered her blessings on the Hamapa.

Made in the USA
Middletown, DE
10 March 2023

26525318R00142